SANTA'S DARK SECRET

To those who are hoping for a Christmas miracle and needing someone to come hard down your chimney, I got you!

Deck the halls, and jingle those balls, baby!

Santa's coming for you, and I hope you're ready when he does!

CONTENT WARNING

Santa's Dark Secret is a 52k word, short dark holiday romance and is not suitable for readers under eighteen years of age.

SANTA'S DARK SECRET CONTAINS

Explicit sexual themes
Coarse language
Stalking
Dubious Consent
Kidnapping

CHAPTER 1

MILA

Okay, I know this is going to sound crazy, but when I was a little girl, only six or seven years old, I saw Santa Claus, and not just in my dreams or in a movie. It was as real as it gets. I saw the big guy in red right there in my living room, muddy boots and all. I'd gotten out of bed late on Christmas Eve to get a glass of milk, and just as I was making my way back to my bedroom, I saw him shimmy his red-suited ass out of my family's fireplace.

Even as a little girl, I'd already heard the rumors on the playground—that the famous present bringer wasn't real. Other kids said that the whole story about Santa and Mrs. Claus, along with their toy-making elves at the North Pole, was nothing but an elaborate ruse to get little boys and girls to fall in line, and I believed those rumors until his big ass appeared in my living room.

Sure, I was losing my tiny mind, realizing that the other kids had been wrong and that Santa was real, but what really surprised me wasn't Santa at all. It was the young boy who followed him out of my fireplace and stood so confidently in my living room.

He was nothing at all like jolly old St. Nick. He was the polar opposite. Dark hair with even darker eyes, and though he was only a boy, there was a strange confidence about him that I will never forget.

They were only there for barely a second, and as Santa put a present under my tree, the boy simply stared at me with a smirk across his full lips, looking at me as though he was just as intrigued as I was. I stood soundlessly in a puddle of milk, barely able to believe what was happening. Then as Santa made his way back to the fireplace, the boy winked, and like a flash of lightning, they were both gone, leaving my little six-year-old mind blown.

I've held a torch for that little boy all my life. Even now as a grown-ass woman, I find myself wondering what he looks like now, what kind of man he turned into, and if that boyish charm grew into an intriguing manly deliciousness.

Insane, right? Yeah, that's exactly what my mother thought too.

The moment I told her I'd seen Santa and a child appear in our living room in the middle of the night, she declared I'd lost my mind. I was clearly acting out due to my parents' recent divorce. I barely had a chance to enjoy Christmas before Mom swept me into a therapist's office to start talking about my hallucinations.

My mother, may she rest in peace, was a fickle woman. Scrap that, she was a cold-hearted bitch. I never got along with her, and truth be told, I think it was her immediate dismissal of what happened that night that started the rocky journey we shared.

All through my childhood and well into my teen years, we fought. I can't remember a single day where there was peace between us, and I was eventually shipped off to live with my father. He, on the other hand, was a delight. I loved my father, and considering how well we got along, I always wished that we had been able to spend more time together. My mother had fought so hard for sole custody just to spite him, but we all would have been so much happier if I had always lived with him.

But just like Mom, my father recently passed away.

Imagine being barely twenty-six and having to bury both your parents within six months of each other. It's been a rough year, to say the least. Mom was taken out by a plastic surgery gone wrong, and my father, the poor bastard, was allergic to healthy food and exercise. His heart attack wasn't exactly the biggest surprise, but that didn't make the pain of losing him any easier.

"Earth to Mila," my friend, Carolina, says, waving her hands in front of my face, snapping me out of my internal misery. We're at our company's ridiculous idea of a Christmas party, and unfortunately, this was a mandatory event. Don't get me wrong, I love a good Christmas party. There's nothing better than watching Jan from

Accounting get wasted off two martinis and slutting it up for Nathan in HR. She's been twerking on him for the past twenty minutes, and as amusing as it is, I'm not feeling it tonight.

"Sorry," I murmur, plastering on a fake smile and lifting my glass to my lips, hoping the cheap wine can somehow dull the ache in my chest—an ache that wasn't put there by the loss of my father only a few short months ago. No, this is a whole new ache. This one is as fresh as they come. "Stuck in my head again."

As of a week ago, I had it all. The perfect boyfriend, Brandon, who I'd hoped was going to propose for Christmas, and a best friend, Amelia, who was my rock through this past year, who held me up when I fell to pieces and was there to wipe my tears when the pain became too much.

But unfortunately for me, my boyfriend was involved in a tragic accident when he slipped and fell straight into my best friend's vagina. It hit me out of nowhere. I was completely blindsided. I'd gone over to Amelia's apartment to surprise her with an early Christmas gift for being such an amazing friend, and turns out, I was the one who got the surprise.

I walked straight into her apartment to see my boyfriend bending her over the couch I sleep on, screwing her brains out.

My heart fell right out of my chest, shattering into a million pieces, and since then, I've been a ghost of the woman I once was. In the space of ten months, I've lost everyone important in my life. My whole support system has crumbled. Mom. Dad. Amelia, and

Brandon.

I do still have Carolina, the woman currently staring at me as though I've lost my mind. While I've known her for a few years, we're just colleagues, and our friendship doesn't often expand outside of working hours.

"Come on," Carolina says. "We're at a party, and even though it's a shitty party with even shittier wine, you should try to have some fun. I know it's been an awful year for you, but tonight is your chance to relax and let off a little steam."

I shrug my shoulders, glancing out at the pathetic excuse of a Christmas party around me. Carolina and I work for a prestigious law firm in New York, and honestly, we're more than lucky to be here, but I'm starting to wonder if any of it is even worth the long, grueling hours. We each finished our law degree, and after interning here, we secured positions. However, the empty promises of promotions are starting to land on deaf ears.

Both of us are at the bottom of the barrel, basically doing all the grunt work for the real lawyers while we idly sit by, waiting for someone to realize that we're more than just paper pushers, and might actually know a thing or two about what we're doing here. I suppose I'm partly to blame for that. I could have pushed myself to be noticed and valued, and I was in that mindset until this year went to shit. Now, I don't even know if I care about this job or the career that could blossom from it. I'm not fulfilled here anymore.

Carolina and I became fast friends and have spent every lunch break—assuming we get one—together for the past four years, and yet, I can't quite figure out why our office friendship hasn't translated into a real outside-of-work friendship. Point is, I'm twenty-six, and I thought at this stage of my life, I would have so much more than just . . . this.

I scoff as I gaze at my friend. "I don't know if I can afford to relax. Every time I do, someone seems to drop dead or stab me in the back."

A cheeky grin rips across Carolina's face. "Well, look at it this way. There's no one left to drop dead or stab you in the back, so what do you have to lose?"

"Damn," I laugh, throwing back what's left of my wine. "You're going in hard tonight."

Carolina laughs. "Let your hair down, Mila. Let's get wasted on the company's dime and have a great night. There are only a few days until Christmas, and from tonight until after New Year's Day, you're officially on break, so who cares if you wake up tomorrow with a killer hangover and a man in your bed? As long as he rocks your world. It's a win-win, girl. What could go wrong?"

I give her a blank stare, and as the idea sits with me, I quickly get on board.

She's right. Why the hell shouldn't I get wasted and fuck around? I like sex just as much as the next girl. I need it. And if Brandon can slut it up for Amelia, then why should I be spending my night moping about some guy when I could be having the time of my life?

"Fuck it," I tell Carolina. "Let's do it."

"YES!" she cheers, holding up her glass. "That's my girl. I thought I'd lost you for a minute."

I roll my eyes, and not a moment later, her arm slips through mine as we make our way back to the bar, determined to make the most of tonight.

An hour later, I stand on a table next to Jan from Accounting, twerking against Nathan from HR while Carolina holds a stack of ones, making it rain for my skank-ass. I haven't got a clue where she would have gotten her hands on a huge stack of dollar bills, but I can't bring myself to care. All that matters is that we're having the time of our lives.

"Rockin' Around The Christmas Tree" blasts from the speakers, and as I sip on cheap wine and let it go straight to my head, I don't dare stop moving. My feet hurt, and as Jan and Nathan start making out right next to me, I figure it's time to call it quits.

Carolina reaches for me as I begin to make my way off the table, and as I move, the bottom of my stiletto catches on the edge of the chair. I can't save myself, and my arms flail as I crash onto the ground, taking Carolina down with me in a fearful fit of laughter.

"Holy fucking shit," she howls, trying to wobble to her feet. "Are you okay?"

All I can do is laugh as I allow her to try and pull me back up, only that's a lot easier said than done, and it ends up taking nearly a whole two minutes before we're both stable on our heels. We fix ourselves one last drink before looping arms and strolling right out the door.

We get halfway down the street before my eyes widen, and I gape at Carolina. "We didn't say goodbye to anyone."

Her eyes widen in horror before we both start laughing all over again. "Oh my God. No wonder they don't want to give us those promotions."

"They're such idiots," I tell her. "We are the best ones in that whole firm. They're lucky to have us."

"Damn straight," she says. "You know Jeremy asked me how to file a subpoena yesterday. Like . . . What the actual fuck? Filing paperwork should come as naturally as wiping your own ass. Tell me, how does that doorknob get promoted over me? Make it make sense."

"Ahhh," I say, holding up a finger as though I've just figured out the solution to the world's problems. "I believe it may have something to do with the slimy, worm-like appendage in his too-tight pants."

"His pants really are too tight. I mean, how does his asshole breathe in there? His ass cheeks are probably permanently squished together."

A smirk lingers on my lips as we dawdle down the street, moving further away from the party and into the cool night. "You think when he farts, the little air bubble has to travel down to his dick and balls, like when girls are sitting down, and it has to escape through the front, and you feel it vibrate through your lips?"

"Oh my God. Yes," Carolina gasps, clutching me tighter as she laughs. "What if he feels it vibrate against his sack? Or . . . Or does it shoot right up the back of his ass crack and escape out through the top of his pants only to get trapped inside the back of his button-down?"

"And then he's just walking around all day wearing his fart?"

"Ughhhhh," Carolina groans in disgust. "I always knew there was a reason why I hated Jeremy so much. He's wearing his farts."

"This needs to be discussed with Nathan as a matter of urgency."

"It absolutely does," Carolina agrees, fishing her phone from her clutch. She fumbles with it for just a moment before swiping her thumb across the screen, and within seconds, Nathan's name appears. She hits call before finding the speakerphone button, and we pause in the middle of the walkway as we listen to the call connecting.

"What the fuck do you want?" A female's voice snaps, quickly followed by a panting gasp. "We're busy."

"Jan?" I ask, listening as hard as my foggy brain can possibly manage. "Is that you?"

"Yes," she groans. "It's me. Now, what do you want?"

Wait . . . Are they fucking?

"Where's Nathan?" Carolina asks, not having caught on quite as fast as I have. "It's a matter of public health. We need to talk to him urgently. Jeremy has been walking around the office wearing his farts."

"What about Jeremy's farts?" Jan asks as a loud slap, slap, slap, slap fills the speakers, putting an image in my head of Nathan's ball sack slamming against Jan's pussy and making me queasy.

"What's that sound?" Carolina asks. "It kinda sounds like—" Her eyes widen in horror, her face quickly draining of color. "Oh shit. Are you two . . . doing it?"

"Trying to," Jan says.

"Oh, nice. Congratulations. You've wanted this for so long. All that twerking must have paid off," Carolina teases before letting out a happy sigh. "How is he doing? Is he living up to all the hype? You know, I heard Nathan was hung like a horse. Is that true?"

"Oh yeah. Tongue action could use a little work, but he knows how to use his equipment. I give him a solid four out of five stars. Oh, you know, when I'm done, you should really give him a try."

"Oh, I don't know about that. The men I screw really need to be on their tongue A-game. But—oh," Carolina's gaze swivels back to me. "You know, Mila doesn't have high expectations of men. I'm sure she'll be willing to give Nathan a good ride. We've been meaning to get her laid tonight."

"What?" I shriek. "I'm not screwing Nathan. He's a million years old and always smells like dirty bath water."

"You sure, love?" Nathan grumbles through the phone, making me realize we're not the only ones with this call on speakerphone. "I'm just about done here. Are you gals still at the party? I could head back there and give you a run for your money. Though, I might need a few minutes. The old boy can't swing back as fast as he used to."

Gross.

Carolina's face scrunches with disgust, and not a second later, her thumb drops down on the hang-up button. "Did that really just happen?" She laughs. "Holy shit. How did Jeremy's dirty farts turn into Nathan's limp dick?"

Tears well in my eyes as laughter claims me, and I crash down against the edge of a fountain, planting my ass on the red tiles. "Nathan should really hire a new HR person so that we can talk to that person about Nathan."

"Yeah, I agree. Let's make it happen."

Carolina lets out a heavy breath and crashes down beside me as she tries to wipe away her tears of laughter, doing what she can not to smudge mascara all over her face, but there's really no point. Her mascara has been smudged since she was making it rain with dollar bills.

I sigh deeply and lean back to graze the water's surface with my fingertips, only to find the top layer iced over. I've always loved the serenity of this place. There's something so soothing about the sound of the running water. You know, when it's not frozen and I don't need to pee.

"I'm sorry we didn't find someone to screw your brains out. At this rate, if you don't get dicked down soon, I'm going to have to get you a Christmas-themed dildo that spurts eggnog when you come." Carolina smirks as she reaches down to touch the ice just as I had, only she goes too far and tips herself off balance. She screams as her ass slides off the edge, her arms flailing for something to grab onto, but it's too late, and the fountain quickly claims her.

I try to save her, quickly reaching for her falling body, but after all that cheap wine, my reflexes aren't exactly on point, and I miss every opportunity to help, leaving me laughing helplessly.

Carolina crashes through the thin layer of ice and sits in the dirty sludge water beneath, gaping at me as though she can't believe how the hell that just happened. The longer she watches me howling with laughter, the more frustrated she becomes, and I can't help but wonder if the cheap wine is dulling her senses because I can only imagine how cold that must be. "You are so not laughing at me right now."

"Oh my god." I cackle harder, the tears rolling down my face as I clutch my stomach. "That was the funniest thing I've ever seen."

"Oh yeah?" She smirks, and like lightning, she reaches forward and grabs my arm, giving it a hard yank until I slide off the edge and crash into the bottom of the dirty fountain right beside her.

"HOLY FUCKING SHIT!" I squeal, sitting in the sludge water like a drowned rat, water trickling off me as I instantly feel the chill in my bones. It's fucking freezing. Swimming in the middle of winter in New York probably isn't the brightest idea.

"You're right," Carolina laughs, splashing dirty fountain ice water over me as her teeth begin to chatter from the cold. "That really was the funniest thing I've ever seen."

"I'm gonna kill you."

"You can try," she says. "But I'm simply too brilliant. You'll miss me too much."

Rolling my eyes, we hastily start climbing out of the fountain before we get hypothermia and everything starts to go numb. My teeth begin to chatter just like Carolina's and the need to get home and in a hot shower becomes my only priority. "Gotta admit, this really isn't how I pictured my night going," I say.

Carolina pulls off her soaking coat, pinching a stray leaf stuck to her soggy thigh, both of us just moments from turning blue. "I know. I'm sorry. I really thought you'd be on your back right now, legs in the air, being railed within an inch of your life."

I let out a heavy sigh, able to picture it so clearly. "Fuck, that actually sounds really good."

Carolina puts her arm around me and we both stare at the offending fountain a moment longer, the two of us violently shaking from the cold. "You know, the best way to heal a broken heart is to let someone else dazzle it."

"I thought the way to get over somebody was to get under somebody else."

"Two things can be true," she laughs before slipping her hand into her soggy pocket and pulling out a single penny. "Here," she continues, handing it to me. "Toss it into the fountain and make yourself a raunchy Christmas wish. Get railed for the holidays. Finish the year off with a literal bang, and when you come back to work in the new year, you'll be fresh as a well-fucked daisy."

My heart starts to race, but that could be the hypothermia setting in.

After I saw Santa and who I assume was his son, I wished for that little boy to return every year. And call me crazy, but I'm almost certain he did. I never saw him again or woke up in the middle of the night to see if he was there, but every single time I'd wake up on Christmas morning, a tiny charm rested on my bedside table.

Sure, some might think it's weird that every Christmas Eve, someone has been coming into my bedroom and leaving me a charm, but I know deep in my gut that it was him—the little boy who winked at me all those years ago.

Even now, I cherish those Christmas charms. I still have every single one of them and have put them together on a bracelet that I'm too afraid to wear for fear I might lose it. But what it really comes back to is that I've wished for him to return every year, and he's done just that.

Only that little boy is no longer a child. He's all grown up now.

I wonder if . . . hmmm.

Maybe I need to ask for something a little . . . more from my mystery Christmas Eve visitor. I already know he's willing to return, but just how far can I push this?

And with that, I close my eyes and toss the little penny into the freezing fountain. "This Christmas, I wish to be dicked down so hard that my knees will shake for weeks after. I wish to be thrown around, flipped over like a pancake, and railed within an inch of my life. I wish to be dragged down my bed only to feel a warm mouth close over my clit and scream as he works me with his skilled tongue."

"Oh, don't forget making him come apart in your mouth," Carolina suggests, her shivers shaking us both.

"Oh yeah. That too," I say through chattering teeth. "But most of all, I wish to come alive, to feel things I've never felt before, and to be screwed so good that nothing will ever compare."

CHAPTER 2

NICK

Ahh, Christmas Eve, the busiest night of the year. For me, at least.

Believe it or not, but I am the big asshole in the red suit. Some may know me as jolly old Saint Nick or Father Christmas, but I'm more commonly known as Santa Claus.

There's a catch, though. I'm not exactly the Santa Claus you're thinking of.

You know the guy you see plastered across the malls every December? The one with the jolly Christmas spirit, rosy cheeks, and the beard? Yeah, that's not me. That's my father, Nick Sr.

He was the one that encompassed the whole Christmas spirit. He gets all hot and bothered for sleigh rides and Christmas carols.

and for the better part of fifty years, he was the greatest Santa Claus to grace the planet. But unfortunately for me, as much as he'd like to think he's invincible, he's not, and only a few short years ago came the dreaded time to retire.

Fuck, he was a cranky bastard leading up to that, but now that he's dedicated his existence to being a thorn in my side, the old man has regained his jolly spirit.

When Dad retired, he handed the literal reins to me, and honestly, I don't know what the fuck he was thinking. I haven't got a Christmassy bone in my body, but I get it. It's a family tradition, and I've known since I was a child that I would one day fill his shoes as the world's next Santa Claus. But fuck, they're big shoes to fill.

The job has been passed down from father to son for countless generations. It was only a matter of time before the title of Santa Claus was thrust upon me, but I had hoped for more time.

I won't lie, it's a lot of responsibility, and while I'm the type to thrive under pressure, there are over two billion kids on the planet who are counting on me to make their Christmas wishes come true. I can't afford to fuck up.

Only problem is, fucking up is one of my favorite things to do.

No pressure, huh?

I'm not exactly a traditional Santa Claus, and it's something my father has worried about since the day I was born. I don't encompass all that holiday cheer that comes so naturally to all the Santas before me.

Quite frankly, I'm the complete opposite. I'm the dark horse of the family. I'm an asshole, and I don't give a shit who knows it. On top of that, I may have a slight sickness . . . a fascination of sorts, one I've worked my ass off to keep concealed.

This job has had one hell of a learning curve, but for as long as I can remember, my old man has been training me, taking me along every Christmas Eve to see what would one day be my responsibility.

As a kid, I loved going with him to see the world outside of the North Pole and to see the joy that this job actually brings. It's one thing just knowing about it, but seeing it in action gave me a whole new appreciation for what we were doing. Though, I'd be lying if I didn't say there were particular perks of the job. Perks that have seen me almost cross the line a million times over. Perks that have more than challenged my self-control.

You see, I may or may not have a slight obsession—a sick, twisted need.

When I was eight years old, the world I'd seen through rose-colored glasses shifted in a big way, and suddenly my purpose of becoming Santa Claus took a back seat, and my sick obsession began to develop.

Mila Morgan.

She was barely six the first time I saw her, but there was something about the innocence in her eyes that drew me in. It was the first time my father had taken me to do the Christmas Eve rounds, and for whatever reason, she was standing right there in the middle of the living room.

I couldn't understand it. She was supposed to be asleep, and for whatever reason, it didn't register that the child inside the home wasn't tucked securely into her bed. None the wiser, we took the journey down the chimney, and when I appeared in the living room to see Mila gaping at me, I instantly became fascinated.

Who was this child, and why the hell could she see me?

I didn't say a word as my father did what he does best and delivered her gift right under the tree as though nothing out of the ordinary was going on, and yet, I couldn't tear my eyes off her. It was the first time I'd seen another human outside of the North Pole, and the warmth in her shell-shocked stare completely captured me.

That very moment kickstarted the next twenty years of obsession. Sure, it started as an innocent crush, but in recent years, it's morphed into something a little more . . . sinister. To put it bluntly, I want to fuck this woman. I want to take her for my own and taste her night after night. There's an animalistic need now, a ferocious hunger to have what I've always wanted.

I watched Mila grow up, returning to her home every year to check in on her, and despite my father's disapproval, I would always leave a small token behind, wanting her to know that I was there. I needed her to remember me, and fuck, she never failed me. She's held on to that memory of the little dark-haired boy who appeared in her living room all those years ago, going as far as to wish for my return every year. I never hesitated because I was desperate to be in her space.

She's a woman now, and I've been starving for her. The way her body has changed, how she's now aware of herself. I'm a fucking animal for Mila Morgan, and I'm not too fucked up to admit that I've been checking in on her a little more often than Christmas allows.

It started just here and there. On her twenty-first birthday, or when she moved to a new apartment. I've always stayed in the background, never getting to touch her, never getting to taste her.

Am I disgustingly aware that I've been stalking this woman? Yes.

Am I aware of how fucking wrong and unhinged it is? Also yes.

Do I give a single fuck? No.

But all that changes this Christmas because Mila didn't just wish for my return this year. She wished for something I've been desperate to give her for years, and there's nothing that'll stop me now.

I sit back in my chair, my feet kicked up on the huge mahogany desk in the office that used to be my father's. There's three hours before I'm due to set off for the biggest night of the year, and yet I'm holed up in my office, rock-fucking-hard, and clutching the printout of Mila's wishes.

I can't help but gaze over it one more time, each of her filthy requests written out with checkboxes that desperately need to be ticked off.

☐ *I wish to be dicked down so hard that my knees will shake for weeks after.*

☐ *I wish to be thrown around, flipped over like a pancake and railed within an inch of my life.*

☐ *I wish to be dragged down my bed only to feel a warm mouth close over my clit and scream as he works me with his skilled tongue.*

☐ *I wish to make him come apart in my mouth.*

☐ *I wish to come alive, to feel things I've never felt before, and to be screwed so good that nothing will ever compare.*

Dicked down so hard that her knees shake? Fuck yes. I am more than happy to do that for her. But what I really can't wait for is to watch as her lips close around my cock, the way her tongue would work up and down my length, how tears would form in her pretty eyes as she forces herself past her gag-reflex to give it to me just right. But fuck, the way I'm going to fall apart in her mouth.

It's as though she's wanted this as much as I have. But that would be selfish, right? I don't just want this for me, I want this for her. She clearly needs it, and who am I to deny a Christmas wish? I'm Santa Claus for fuck's sake. It's literally my job to give her what she wants. And tonight, that's exactly what I'll do.

I hope she's ready for me.

My cock becomes painful, and I can't help but reach beneath my desk and slide my hand inside my pants, fisting my hard length. My gaze remains locked on the words of Mila's wishes as I slowly begin working myself, my fist pumping up and down. I picture the way I will finally taste her, how I would spread those creamy thighs and close my mouth over her desperate cunt.

Fuck, the way she will squirm for me. The way she will arch her back off her bed and cry for more. She's going to be perfect.

My fist tightens, and I work myself faster and harder, my thumb roaming over my tip and making my hips jolt with desperation.

Fuck, that's good. I need so much more.

I need her warm cunt to slide into. I need to fucking destroy her for anybody else. Take her as deep as she'll allow. Fuck her all night long. Hard. Fast. Deep. In every fucking position known to man. I want to make her sweat, but most of all, I need to make her scream.

Goddamn, I'm going to fall apart just thinking about it.

My pace kicks up, and knowing I'm about to be called to get tonight's show on the road soon, I make it quick. I fuck my hand, knowing this has got nothing on how sweet it would be to feel Mila's walls spasming around me, but I don't let up until I finally come, shooting my hot load into my hand. After all, I can't mess up the red suit.

My body jolts as I finish emptying myself, my jaw clenching as the satisfaction rockets through my body. But the relief only lasts a moment. I've been wanting this for too long for the need to dissipate. No amount of jerking off has ever done the trick. The only thing that ever brings relief is her, and until now, I've never laid a finger on her. But that's about to change.

Cleaning myself up, I fix my pants and get up from my desk, grabbing my red suit jacket off the back of my chair. Mila's list of

Christmas wishes crumple, as I shove it into my pocket, and just as I pull my jacket around me and button up the famous red suit, a knock sounds at my door.

"Coming," I mutter, reaching for the handle and swinging the door open. My father stands in the open doorway with his executive assistant Frederick. And no, his helpers aren't elves. They are regular people like me and Mila. I never really understood where the whole elves thing came into play, but once whispers of Santa's little helpers hit the modern world, they ran with it. I suppose little magical elves aren't so far-fetched considering the reindeer farm right outside my kitchen window.

"Santa," Frederick says with a chipper tone and a wide smile that makes me want to knock out his two front teeth.

I let out a sigh, cutting him off before he has a chance to say whatever he came to tell me. "It's Nick, Fred. I don't know how many times I need to remind you."

A sheepish look crosses his face. "Sorry, Sa—Nick. Old habits die hard. I don't think I'll ever get used to calling you by your name. It makes me feel all . . . squirmy."

"Squirmy?" I question, arching a brow as I step back into my office and grab my belt, all while my father silently watches me from Frederick's side, clearly wondering if he's made the right decision to retire. Though I managed the last two years without fucking up, so I think I'm good.

"Yes, Sir. Squirmy," he says, as I nod toward the corridor, indicating for my father and Frederick to walk with me. "Now, getting on with important matters. The list has been checked and double-checked. However, there have been a few last-minute additions to the naughty list. I recommend taking one final glance at it before you take off."

"Will do," I mutter, forcing myself to keep my mind off Mila and get serious about what I'm supposed to be doing tonight. "How are my reindeer looking?"

My father takes it upon himself to answer this one. He's always had such a soft spot for our furry friends. "All good, son, but you know they also get a little . . . squirmy on Christmas Eve. I believe they're eager to get going."

A small smile pulls at my lips. My father isn't the only one who has a soft spot for our reindeer. They truly are magnificent animals, and for the most part, they were my best friends growing up. After all, there are not many other kids to play with out here. "No surprise there," I say, glancing back toward Frederick. "Gifts?"

"I have a team still loading them into the sack. Maybe another hour or so and it'll be ready to go."

"Perfect."

I start heading toward the vault that houses the list, determining who's been good this year, and I smile knowing damn well that Mila would have easily found her way onto the naughty list for the Christmas wish she sent my way. Only that's the kind of naughty I like most.

Frederick gets on his way, overseeing all the ins and outs of my workshop, and just when I expect my father to follow me into the vault, he clutches my elbow and pulls me aside. "Are you ready? It's a big night ahead."

"As ready as I can be, Dad. You've spent the last twenty years preparing me for every type of situation. I know what I'm doing."

"I know you do, but . . ." He lets out a heavy sigh. "I'm concerned about you, Nicholas. If you remember, I oversaw the Christmas wishes this year. I saw what that girl wished for, and I don't want you to get distracted. You have an important night ahead of you, and I know you've always had a certain . . . fascination with this girl."

Well fuck. I was expecting a lot of things to come out of his mouth but certainly not that. I wonder how Mila would feel learning that the jolly old Father Christmas she grew up with saw just how filthy her desires truly are.

"Honestly, Dad. I'm good," I lie, stepping up to the door of the vault and putting in the code. "Last year, I had an extra few hours up my sleeve. I even stopped for a concert appearance in Sydney. Blew a few people's minds."

"I don't want you rushing just to try and prove a point," he reprimands. "That's how kids get missed. Take your time, and try to remember that Christmas is all about spreading joy."

A smirk pulls at my lips as the vault door begins to open. I'll sure as fuck be spreading something, though I can't guarantee that it'll be joy.

"I've got it all under control, pops. You don't need to worry this year. I know my priorities."

He arches a brow, and the jolly old man the rest of the world is used to seeing disappears, left with the stern father who raised me to be the perfect carbon copy of him. Only, I'm not quite sure it worked. I'm nothing like him.

"Do you?" he challenges.

Fuck. I hate when he gets like this. It's as though he can see right through me to the dark little soul hidden within. He's always known I was different, but deep down, he knows he can rely on me to get the job done. I won't be letting anyone down tonight.

"Of course. I'm not going to let you down, and I'm not about to let any single one of the two billion kids down either."

"Two and a half billion."

I resist rolling my eyes. "Why don't you take the evening off? Make some hot cocoa and chill by the fireplace with Mom. Maybe try to remember that you're retired, and while I may be the black sheep of the family, you handed me the keys to the castle because you knew I was ready."

Dad lets out a heavy sigh. "I suppose you're right."

"I know I am."

"Fine, I'll go spend the evening with your mother." He gives me a tight smile and claps me on my shoulder before turning and waddling away, leaving me to focus on the vault.

As I move to step over the threshold, my father's booming tone rings out again. "Oh, Nicholas?"

Stopping in the middle of the doorway, I turn back to meet my father's dark gaze. "Try to remember to enjoy yourself."

A fond smile stretches across my lips. "I will, pops," I murmur, always having hated this sentimental shit. "I'll check in with you in the morning. Tell you all about it."

"Be sure that you do," he says, and with that, he finally turns away to hopefully take his ass home.

With his stark warning still flashing in my mind, I step over the threshold of the vault and hit a few buttons on the other side to close the door behind me. I don't know what it is about checking the list that feels so personal, but every time I do, I require absolute silence and concentration. There's nothing I hate more than being disturbed in here, and knowing time is running out before I'm due to leave, I don't want a single interruption.

I give myself an hour, going over every single name and making sure I have them committed to memory. After all, once I take off, there's no way for me to double back and check if I forget. I've got one shot to get it right, and I'm not the type of man to fuck things up.

Once I'm sure I have the nice and naughty lists fully memorized, I make my way over to the side of the vault to the massive floor-to-ceiling windows that overlook the workshop below. I've grown up here, and yet the sheer size of this place still blows my mind. There's always a constant flood of helpers rushing around down there, but on Christmas Eve, it's pure madness.

The last of the presents are being loaded into the shoot that takes them directly to my sack, and the very moment the last present arrives, the sack will be loaded onto the sleigh.

I give myself a minute to take it all in, making sure I'm truly prepared for the night ahead, and before I know it, I'm making my way outside.

People stop me in the hallways to wish me luck for my big night. If only they knew I was more excited about fucking Mila into oblivion rather than performing my saintly duties. But I suppose that's something I should keep to myself.

Heading out into the chilly December night, I find my reindeer already harnessed and ready to go, lined up perfectly. Making my way toward them, I grab a bucket and fill it with water before making my way down the line, offering them each one last drink before we go.

They don't really need it. Many homes will have carrots and water left out for them, and to be honest, by the time we return home, every single one of them will have a stomach ache. But that's their own fault for eating so many damn carrots. I swear, these fuckers don't know when to stop. Just because something is put in front of your face, doesn't mean you need to eat it.

Except pussy. More specifically Mila's. If that's in front of my face, I can guarantee it will be eaten. No doubt about it. Perhaps the reindeer need a little more leniency. I suppose I understand their carrot addiction.

With the list thoroughly checked and the reindeer ready to go,

I make my way over to my sleigh, climbing in and getting ready for the trip ahead.

"Ahem." A throat clears beside me, and I glance to my left to see Frederick standing in the snow, my Santa hat clutched in his hand. "Forgetting something?"

"No, I made a point not to bring that with me."

He gives me a blank stare.

"What more do you want from me? I'm already wearing the red pants, the suspenders, and the fucking jacket. Do I really have to wear the hat as well?"

"Santa isn't Santa without the hat," he tells me. "But you know I don't have to remind you that any piece of Santa's suit must be returned to head office, and between you and me, your father will be checking in during the night, and if he finds you left without the hat—"

"Fuck." I snatch the goddamn hat out of his hand and throw it into the bottom of the sleigh. "Happy now?"

"Ecstatic," he chimes before waving his hand toward the big, wide world. "Have at it, Santa. Go make some wild Christmas wishes come true."

I grin as I take the reins. "That's exactly what I intend to do."

CHAPTER 3

MILA

Reaching up onto my tippy toes, I hang the final ornament on my Christmas tree. I know it's a bit late to be doing this shit considering it's already Christmas Eve. I should have had it done weeks ago, but there's no time quite like the present. Besides, if my mystery Christmas visitor is really coming tonight, then I can't risk disappointing him.

I want everything to be perfect.

Scrap that. I need it to be perfect.

Ahh shit. Who am I kidding? This is truly insane.

Maybe I've made this whole thing up in my head. Maybe Mom was right to send me to a therapist as a kid. Do I really believe that I threw a penny into a fountain and all of a sudden, Santa's filthy son is going to come down my chimney and fuck me until I scream?

Yes. Yes, indeed. I do believe it. Though it leaves me with so many questions.

First off, I don't have a chimney anymore. After Dad died, our old family home was sold, and I moved into a little apartment to be closer to work. However, I do have a fire escape, so I assume he could sneak in through there. But also, if this is actually going to happen, I've never been more thankful that my neighbors have gone away for the holidays. The last thing I need is for Greg, Allison, and their three kids to hear my world get rocked by a fictional man . . . or maybe he isn't fictional. I really don't know at this point. Either way, if and when he comes, I'll be ready.

Second issue on my agenda. What if this guy really isn't who I think he is? Sure, he must be somewhat of a good man if he comes to fulfill my Christmas wish every year and leaves me a charm for my bracelet. But what if it's not actually Santa's son who's been coming all these years? What if it's actually Santa and I just asked him to come down my throat?

Holy shit. What have I done?

Nerves pound through my chest and settle deep in my gut. Am I about to be thoroughly fucked by Santa Claus? What is Mrs. Claus going to think about that? Shit. If that's the case, I hope he's been working out. I don't want to give the old man a heart attack. But also, I hope he's trimmed his beard for the occasion. I want to be left shaking and exhausted, not left with a beard rash on my pussy and the new title of being an adulterous whore.

Well, I suppose that would make Santa Claus the adulterous whore, right? Not me. Though, it would explain why he's always so jolly. I would be too if I had women all around the world getting me off.

Oh God. Why am I now picturing Santa getting his dick sucked?

Damn it. I wonder if my old therapist's number is somewhere buried in all of Mom's old things.

I really hope this goes the way I want it to because not being thoroughly fucked is out of the question. I just need to get it, him, out of my system once and for all, and then I'm sure I'll wake up in the morning ready to move on with my life.

I'll be able to forget about my mystery Christmas Eve visitor, find myself a billionaire who isn't going to cheat on me with my best friend, and finally settle down. Perhaps buy a home and start a family, have a few kids who I won't call crazy if they happen to see Santa Claus. Maybe even add a dog to the equation. Sounds absolutely blissful to me.

With the tree finally finished, I take a few steps back to look at it from a distance, and as the lights twinkle in the darkness, the nostalgia hits me like a tidal wave.

For a moment, my chest aches with memories of the past. Having a mother to harp on my choice of dress. A father to wrap his arms around me and tell me how proud he is of me. A boyfriend to bring Chinese food over and help decorate the apartment, and to wake up next to him on Christmas morning. A best friend to show up to dinner with a bottle of good wine and a million hilarious stories to lighten the awkward conversation.

I suppose this year will be different. While everyone else's families are coming together for the holidays, I'll just be here all alone.

I've never been so alone in all my life.

Heartbreak infects me, and I do what I can to shake it off. This is my first Christmas alone, and I'm terrified of the swarm of emotions that will come tomorrow. Perhaps Carolina will let me crash her family Christmas this year. Though if my filthy wishes come true overnight, I'm hoping that getting out of bed and actually walking around will be almost impossible.

Grabbing the almost-empty box of decorations, I pull out the long garland and figure out where the hell to put it before placing a few figurines up on my shelf and hanging a few extra lights.

Once my small home looks positively Christmassy, I make my way into the kitchen and pull out a few cookies and a glass of milk before presenting them nicely on the counter. I find myself staring at them for a moment. This is exactly what I used to do as a kid. I haven't done it in a while because this was all for Santa. Only tonight, it's not Santa I'm expecting.

Will my knight in shining Christmas decorations be down with the whole milk-and-cookies thing? Or is a man who's potentially capable of fucking me into oblivion in need of something a little more exciting? I'm going to go with option B. He wants the good shit.

Grabbing the glass of milk, I pour it straight down the sink, cringing at the wastage, but let's be real. If I were to drink that whole glass of milk, I'd spend the night in the bathroom instead of on my back. After quickly washing the glass, I put it back in the cupboard before switching it out for a shot glass.

I'm a chick drinker and never really advanced from the late teen sweet drinks like Smirnoff or moscato. I can tolerate a cheap wine if it's free, but apart from that, if it doesn't taste like a watermelon and a passionfruit made passionate sex on top of a pile of liquid sugar, I don't want it. However, after Dad passed, I raided his alcohol cabinet and took anything that looked expensive, and I suppose tonight, it's finally going to pay off.

Reaching up into my cupboard, I wrap my fingers around the neck of a bourbon bottle before hesitating and reaching for the whiskey instead. Striding back to the counter, I fill the shot glass, and instead of putting the whiskey back in the cupboard, I leave it out, not sure about how many hits he might want to take. But I'm capping him at four. I won't tolerate him getting whiskey dick tonight, not when I've been needing this so badly.

Certain that I have everything prepared, I double-check that the deadbolt on the door is locked before checking the few windows around my apartment. I rarely open them, but I still find myself checking them every single night.

With everything as it should be, I turn my attention to my bedroom, and nerves instantly flood me, but I swallow them down, determined to see this through. It's not just what I intend to do with him that makes me nervous, but the fact I'm actually going to meet the man who's plagued my mind for so many years. Questions I've had all my life will finally be answered, and I can't wait.

My life has been such a clusterfuck lately that I deserve this, even if it's level ten messed up.

Striding into my bedroom, I find the red lingerie set chilling on my bed and a wide grin stretches across my face. It's perfect. When I saw it in the store yesterday, I couldn't resist picking it up. Even if my mystery man doesn't show up, it's a purchase I'll cherish for years to come.

I don't hesitate peeling off my clothes and picking up the lingerie, starting with the bralette and setting it into place before reaching behind me and fixing the clasp at my back. I can't help but stare in the mirror, watching as the outfit slowly comes together.

The bralette is a deep red lace with minimal coverage, but my small B cups don't exactly need the support. The lace is soft against my skin, and with the spray tan I got just for the occasion, the color truly pops. The matching thong is just as cute, and as I slide the lacey material up my legs, the butterflies in my belly take flight.

I settle it into place, loving how it sits against my skin. It's absolutely perfect and I've never felt so sexy in a piece of lingerie before. Finishing off the look, I take the garter belt and clasp it around my body.

It's everything.

I absolutely love it.

The matching set is perfect and fits me just right, accentuating the slight curves of my body. The deep red isn't exactly the bright festive red we're all used to, but it'll more than get the job done tonight.

Finishing off the look, I slip my feet into a pair of nude heels before spritzing my favorite perfume across my body. I touch up some lipstick and let my hair down, watching as it falls into soft waves down my back.

The nerves get stronger, but I'm in it for the long haul now. There's no turning back. No giving up. I need to see this through, and what's more, I need to feel my body come alive.

My ex and I had a great sex life. We were always going at it, and while he wasn't exactly the best I ever had, he was capable of giving me what I needed, which only leaves me with more questions. Was I not enough? Was he not satisfied with me? Why did he feel the need to screw my best friend?

Ugh. I can't think about that tonight. This is about me, and that asshole is not going to ruin this for me too.

Moving around my bedroom, I stand in front of my full-length mirror, taking in the overall look, and I couldn't be happier. I hope like hell my mystery Christmas Eve visitor likes what he sees because if he doesn't, I think it will break my heart.

With only one last Christmas tradition left, I make my way into my small walk-in closet and reach up onto my highest tippy toes to the very top shelf. I feel around blindly until my fingers swipe across the small velvet box, and I quickly grab it, pulling the box down as a sweet fondness floods my chest.

I open the small box, revealing my charm bracelet, full of the little charms that he's left on my bedside table over the last twenty years. There's a little reindeer, a sleigh, a Santa hat, and a Christmas tree. There's a snow globe, a Mrs. Claus, a present, and so many more. Anything Christmas related, and I can guarantee there's a little charm right here on this bracelet to represent it. But my all-time favorite one is the little gingerbread man winking back at me.

Placing it down on my bedside table just like I've done every other year, I arrange it so that the little gingerbread man is front and center, and with everything just the way I want it, I drop down on my bed and prepare myself for what could only be the best night of my entire life.

CHAPTER 4

NICK

I'm fucking wrecked, but nothing is about to stop me from finally fulfilling Mila's wish. I've been around the globe and made sure to check every last name off my list. Not to mention, I achieved it in record time, leaving me more than enough time to make Mila's legs shake.

I've been waiting for this for years. During my childhood years, all I wanted was for her to wake up again. To see and remember that I was real, not a figment of her imagination. Then during my teen years, I started to wonder what it'd be like to kiss her, to feel how her skin felt beneath my fingers. But once those late teen years hit, it was fucking over for me.

I wanted her. I wanted to run my tongue up her thighs and taste her. I wanted to hear the way she would cry out when I made her come. I wanted it all.

Up until tonight, I've resisted. But not anymore.

Tonight, she finally gets exactly what she's been craving, and I get fucking everything.

Parking my sleigh on the rooftop of Mila's New York apartment complex, I make my way down the fire escape before glancing back over my shoulder and making sure the reindeer aren't going to cause any problems.

Most of them will probably take the chance to nap, but a handful of them are just adolescents on their first trip and can't exactly be trusted. It's been one hell of a night for them, so I'm banking on the fact that they're exhausted. They can rest up now and have regained just enough energy to get us back to the North Pole before sunrise.

With every step I take down the fire escape, the exhaustion from the night begins to wear off, and I'm filled with desperate adrenaline. Just the thought of what's about to happen makes my heart race in a way it never has before. I've dreamed of this moment, pictured how it would happen a million different times, and there's no doubt in my mind that how this actually plays out is going to be a million times better than I could have ever imagined.

It's only a short descent to Mila's apartment, and my quick steps eat up the distance in no time. Before I know it, I'm jimmying her living room window open. This whole breaking and entering thing would have been a shitload easier if she had been at her old family home. I could have shot myself down the chimney like I usually do, but I get it. Not a lot of homes come equipped with a fireplace anymore, and if they do, they're electrical. We Santas have had to evolve and find new and exciting ways to be criminal masterminds. My personal favorite entrance is through the doggy door. Don't ask me how I manage it though. It's not pretty, especially when that doggy door belongs to an angry Great Dane named Diesel. I almost lost my manhood with that one.

My booted feet come down in Mila's apartment, and the moment I close the window behind me, her familiar scent fills the air. I can't help but breathe it in, pacifying the obsessive demon within me, but it won't last long, not now that I know what's on offer.

I haven't been through her new apartment before, so I take a moment to glance around, familiarizing myself with her space. It's small, much smaller than anything I've ever pictured for her. I've always seen her in a big home with space for a family pet to run, or a big kitchen to mess up every night. But here? I don't know. There's no way in hell she's happy here.

She's lived in a few different homes growing up. Her mom always had her moving around through her teen years. She was always in modest homes with small yards, but when she moved in with her dad, I could see how much she loved it there by the homemade cookies on the kitchen counter and the mess that was always left behind from it. Sugar and flour were scattered from one end of the kitchen to the other, and judging by the way the flour was up against the walls, I can only assume their baking adventures had turned into a food fight at some point. It was the same every year, right up until this past Christmas.

I suppose everything is different for Mila now. This would be her first Christmas without her parents. Though last I checked, she had a douche of a boyfriend, but I suspect by her desperate need to be railed tonight, that boyfriend is no longer in the picture. Or the fucker has no idea how to please my girl.

The thought has a wicked grin spreading across my face. But to be completely honest, even if Mila was in her bedroom right now with the love of her life cozied up beside her, that wouldn't stop me from fucking her until she screams. Her boyfriend would simply have to watch me rail his woman within an inch of her life. Perhaps he might learn a few things in the process. Makes for an awkward Christmas day between them. However, that's not my problem. I'm here to fulfill her every wish tonight, not his.

Noticing a shot glass and a bottle of whiskey on the kitchen counter, I take the four small strides from the living room window into the kitchen and collect the shot glass in my big hand. It's down the hatch in seconds, and I don't hesitate to pour myself another shot, welcoming the sweet burn as it travels down my throat.

It's been one hell of a big night, and if I had to see another glass of spoiled milk that's been sitting out all night, I surely would have thrown up. There's only so much milk a man can tolerate. My old man was all about drinking that shit. He has an iron stomach. On the other hand, I pour that shit down the kitchen sink. No one has time to drink two billion glasses of milk in one night. However, the cookies I can always make time for.

The apartment looks as though Christmas has thrown up all over it, and while I've never really cared for decorations, I appreciate the effort she put in. As my gaze continues sweeping Mila's home, taking in the ornaments on the tree and the little figurines left scattered on her small coffee table, my stare lands upon her open bedroom door.

A wave of excitement pulses through me, knowing she's right inside that room. Right there waiting for me. Just the thought gets me hard.

Forgetting everything else, I make my way toward her, quickly eating up the steps across her living room until I finally reach her bedroom. I hover at her door, my big shoulders almost brushing both frames as I take her in, sprawled across her bed with the soft moonlight shining through her window and illuminating her petite figure.

She's fucking breathtaking.

Her body is perfectly gift-wrapped just for me, her soft curves decorated in a crimson lingerie set. She's fast asleep with one arm shoved under her pillow and her hair spread out across the top, and despite the chilly night, she lays across the top of the blanket. A pair of heels are secured to her feet and while I know that can't be comfortable, I love it all the same.

She did this just for me.

My cock twitches in my pants, and a groan rumbles through my chest, desperation quickly turning my hardening cock into a steel rod. I can't wait to touch her, but I intend to take my time.

Moving deeper into her bedroom, I undo the black belt around my waist, letting it drop to the carpet and waiting to see if the noise will wake her, but after twenty years of visiting her in her sleep, it's no secret this woman sleeps like the living dead.

My boots are silent on the floor as I move around the side of her bed, slowly pulling off my big red coat and tossing it toward the armchair in the corner of her room. I'm left with suspenders over my shoulders to hold up the pants that barely contain my erection, but I get the feeling she'd want me to leave them on—at least for now.

Standing at the side of her bed, I see her Christmas charm bracelet on her bedside table, filled with the little mementos I've given her for each of my visits, and just seeing it there fills me with a strange warmth I've never experienced with anyone else but her. Every year it's the same, and I'm fucking addicted to it.

Mila shifts in her sleep, putting herself straight on her stomach and hitching her knee up high, unintentionally spreading those creamy thighs, and the need within me skyrockets.

Fuck, she's simply stunning.

My cock flinches, begging for relief, and I can't wait a moment longer.

Reaching for the front of my pants, I release the buttons and slip my hand inside. I take my straining cock, giving a firm squeeze before finally freeing it and gritting my teeth as the pleasure rocks through me.

I step into the side of Mila's bed and as my fist begins pumping up and down my thick cock, my thumb roaming over my tip and making my hips jolt with a ferocious need, I reach down toward her bed, my gaze locked on the perky globes of her ass in her crimson thong with the slightest hint of her pussy peeking between her spread thighs.

I've waited so long to feel her skin beneath mine, and as my fingertips connect with her ankle, a shiver sails right down my spine. I close my eyes for just a moment as I feel the hunger ripping through my body, and when I reopen them, I watch my fingers brush up her leg with a laser-sharp stare.

A soft moan slips from her lips, and my gaze falls to her beautiful face as she begins to stir, but it's not enough to completely wake her. My fingers continue traveling up, moving from her knee and up the outside of her thigh, enticing another moan from her, this one filled with a little more heat.

Mila's eyelids begin to flutter, and my heart booms rapidly in my chest, needing to have her eyes locked on mine once again, just like she did all those years ago.

That's right, baby. Open your eyes for me.

My fingers continue higher on her thigh. When I can't take it a moment longer, I slip my hand between her legs, cupping her sweet pussy. I feel her warmth and groan low, clutching my cock tighter and willing myself not to come.

Fuuuck. I need her.

Mila sucks in a breath, grinding against my hand, and I cup her tighter, massaging her clit through her crimson thong. When she finally opens her eyes, her hooded gaze sails over my body, starting at my face before slowly trailing down my chest and abs. When she takes in the sight of my straining cock, she licks her lips, hunger blossoming in her eyes as she rises up onto her elbow.

"It's really you," she whispers into the moonlit room, looking at me in disbelief. I thought she would be scared or gasp at the sight of a strange man in her home, but it's as though her soul recognizes mine. "I knew you'd come."

"You wished for me to come and fuck you until your knees shake, Mila. Of course I came," I growl, watching the way she watches me and giving her the show she's been waiting for as my thumb roams over the tip of my cock. "There'll be time to talk later. I've waited years to feel your pretty lips around my cock. Don't keep me waiting a second longer, Mila. Worship me on your knees and show me how well you take me."

Mila doesn't hesitate to slide off the edge of the bed, her bare knees spread against the hardwood floor, and as she looks up at me through her thick lashes, her eyes shine with the deepest, raw excitement. Her tongue rolls over her bottom lip again, leaving it shimmering with saliva, and I instinctively inch toward her, wondering if I'm going to have to guide her through this. But without a single ounce of hesitation, her hand comes down over mine on my cock and she instantly takes over. Her fist is firm, but not too tight, which is exactly how I like it, and as she slowly begins working her way to my tip, my knees threaten to give out. Just the feel of her touch is too much, but when she slightly rises up on her knees, and I feel her warm breath brushing across the tip of my cock, I almost fucking lose it.

I can't keep my eyes off her. I've anticipated this moment for years, but nothing could possibly compare to how it actually feels. Mila doesn't take her eyes off me as she leans in, and when she opens her mouth and her tongue flicks over my tip, I fucking crumble, reaching behind her and knotting my hand into her long hair.

"Yes, Mila. Fuck me with your mouth. Take me deep, baby."

Her eyes glisten with the challenge as she opens wide and leans into me, taking me right in the back of her throat as her fist continues pumping up and down my thick length. Her mouth closes firmly around me, and as her tongue roams over my velvety skin, my hips jolt.

I tighten my hold on the back of her hair as she looks up at me with those bright green eyes, desperate to please me. "Just like that," I rumble.

Mila's cheeks hollow out as she sucks, her head bobbing back and forth as her fist follows her movements, her tongue not letting up for a single second. It's fucking magical. I thought I was coming here to make her legs shake, but fuck, she's the one bringing me to my knees. I should have known better. Her wish was to make me come undone, to make me fall apart in her mouth, and that's exactly what she intends to do.

Mila moans as she works me with her tongue, and the vibrations rock through me, leaving me in a fucking chokehold, but when her free hand reaches up and cups my balls, I just about lose it. She cups me firmly, her fingers gently massaging, and fuck, it's the sweetest pleasure I've ever felt.

She doesn't let up, working me as though she already knows exactly what she's doing to me. Her confidence is like nothing I've ever experienced, and I can't hold on a moment longer. "Fuck, Mila."

Her eyes shimmer as she pushes herself further, taking me deeper into the back of her throat. When she begins to hum, I do just that, letting myself fall to fucking pieces as I come hard into her sweet mouth, emptying myself until there's nothing left to give.

She doesn't ease up on me, continuing to pump her fist up and down my length as the intense orgasm rips through me, her fingers rolling over my tightened balls until my knees physically begin to fail me.

I have no choice but to pull her back, the intensity is too much, and as she releases me, I can't help but watch her. Mila sits back on her heels, not tearing her eyes off mine for even a second as she makes a show of dragging her thumb across her bottom lip.

She offers me her hand, and I don't hesitate to help her to her feet, only she moves in closer, those blazing green eyes locked on mine. "Tell me, did I live up to your expectations?"

Fuck me. This woman.

I simply nod, more than enjoying being in her presence. "You exceeded them."

"Good," she murmurs, placing her hand against my chest as the electricity burns between us. "Because I have expectations of my own, and if you don't start making me scream soon, then you'll be tied to that chair and forced to watch me as I do it myself. I've waited long enough for you. I'm ready now, and I don't want to wait a moment longer."

A wicked grin stretches across my face.

I love nothing more than a good challenge, and if Mila Morgan says she's ready to be fucked right now, then who the hell am I to keep her waiting? Only, if she thinks she's running this show, she's got another thing coming.

CHAPTER 5

MILA

My chest heaves as I try to catch my breath, still tasting his cum in the back of my throat. I've never felt so alive. The moment he touched me, my body filled with electricity, and all that mattered was pleasing him. I needed to make him come. I needed to feel the way he fell apart for me, and damn it, that's exactly what he did.

I had him right where I wanted him, completely crippled under my touch. He gave me everything and was at my mercy, and it was the single best moment of my life. I've never felt so beautiful. So desired. Everything else faded away, and all that mattered was us. But now, there's a shift in the air, and as my chest rises and falls right in front of him, I realize that I was a fool to assume I had any real control here.

This is his game, and I'm just a piece for him to play with as he sees fit. But there's a thrill in that, an excitement that builds deep in my core, promising that this is about to be the best night of my life. He inches closer to me, his arm locking around my waist and pulling me in hard against his chest, and I feel his rock-hard cock against my stomach.

I'm already addicted to his smell. It's as though he just stepped straight out of the woods, but I suppose that's what you get when you live in the North Pole . . . assuming that part of the story is actually true. It seems there's still so much I don't actually know about this man. Hell, I don't even know his name. But the red coat on my armchair, the boots, and the red pants suggest that maybe he's Santa after all, which leaves me with more questions than I started with, but right now, all that matters is the feel of his arm locked around my waist.

"Your body belongs to me," he rumbles, a slight accent to his deep tone. "I'm going to take you Mila. I'm going to spread you apart and claim your sweet little cunt over and over until you physically can't give anymore. Do you understand me? I won't stop until you beg me to."

Oh God.

I swallow hard and nod, the anticipation building rapidly in my chest. "I don't think you understand just what you're getting yourself into."

He scoffs as though the idea of not knowing how every second of this is going to pan out is absurd to him, and not a moment later, his hand is on my ass, hauling me up into his strong arms. My legs wrap around his muscled waist as my arm locks around his neck.

My heated gaze remains locked on his, and fuck, he's absolutely everything I've ever thought he'd be. The little dark-haired boy I saw all those years ago is now this dark-haired beast who knows how to make all my sexual fantasies come true. Everything about him is huge. His height, his shoulders, his hands . . . and especially his cock. I could barely fit my mouth around him, but I'm not one to back down from a challenge, so I did what I could to make it happen, even if it meant sacrificing my throat to the BJ gods.

Every single inch of him is covered with toned muscle. It's as though he spends every other night of the year chained to his home gym. There's no doubt about it—this man is absolutely gorgeous. His sharp, stubbled jaw makes the butterflies in the pit of my stomach take flight, but his dark, hooded eyes are so intense that my pussy throbs.

"I have pictured taking you in every way physically possible, Mila. I've pictured your lips wrapped around my cock, the taste of your sweet little cunt, and even how far I could stretch your ass, and no matter how wild you are, how intense or good you are, no matter if you bring me to my fucking knees, I will always give you what you need. So trust me when I tell you that I know exactly what I'm getting myself into. It's you, my sweet Mila, who doesn't understand.

But it's okay, I will ease you into it."

Ease me into it? Oh fuck. Just how hard is he going to fuck me? Don't tell me he's one of those guys who's going to hang me from the ceiling fan and play out his weird, kinky fantasies. I mean, sure, I'll play along, and he'll probably make me feel some kind of way, but it's not really what I'm hoping to get out of tonight. Though something tells me I'm dead wrong on that one. This delicious piece of man meat right here knows exactly what I need and how to get me there. There's no doubt about it.

"Do your worst," I murmur, holding his intense stare. "Make me scream, but first, what's your name? I need to know exactly what name I should be screaming when you make me come."

A cocky smirk pulls at the corner of his lips, and it makes my heart boom in my chest. He truly is the most gorgeous man I have ever seen. "Scream for your god, baby. He's the only one who can save you now."

With that, my mystery Christmas Eve visitor walks around to the bottom of my bed and sets me down on the edge before collecting both of my wrists. I watch him with curiosity as he slips his hand into his pocket and pulls out a red satin cloth that instantly sends a wicked thrill pulsing right through to my core.

He ties the satin fabric around my wrists, and I swallow hard as he pulls it into a secure knot and takes a step back to survey his handiwork.

His dark stare penetrates mine, and with nothing but the

moonlight shining against his muscular body, my mouth waters.

"Lay back, Mila. Hands above your head."

Hunger fills me, and I do exactly what I've been told, slowly laying back onto my bed with my bound wrists above my head.

"Spread those pretty thighs. Show me what I've been waiting for."

Again, I don't hesitate, bringing my feet up onto the bottom of the mattress before slowly spreading them wide as though offering him up a buffet. "Take me," I beg him, my stare locked and loaded on him. "It's all yours."

He clenches his jaw and fists his cock, squeezing it hard, and just when I expect him to step into me, tear my thighs from my body and fuck me hard, he drops to his knees at the end of my bed.

Oh, fuck yes.

Taking my spread thighs, he wraps his arms around them and drags me the rest of the way down the bed until my ass is barely hanging off the mattress. My legs hook over his wide shoulders, and he quickly buries his head between my thighs, closing his mouth over my thong-covered pussy.

He inhales deeply, and I groan just as he sucks my clit right through my sheer underwear, already driving me wild. He pulls back just an inch, his fingers slipping under the edge of my thong and pulling it aside just enough to expose my needy cunt. "Mmm, you're ready for me."

The only response my body is capable of is to clench my pussy, begging to be touched, and within seconds, I feel his fingertips slowly trailing over my clit. It tickles, but fuck does it feels good, and as he takes them lower, I suck in a breath. The anticipation of what's to come is surely going to kill me.

Finding my entrance, he teases me for a moment before leaning back in and closing his warm mouth over my clit, his tongue rolling over the sensitive bud, and just as a loud groan tears from deep in my chest, he slides two thick fingers inside of me.

"Oh fuck," I pant, arching my back right off the mattress.

He hits the spot straight away, and my eyes roll, but when he curls his fingers inside me and begins to massage, I become a squirming mess on my bed. He sucks and nips my clit, the intensity shooting from zero to one hundred in the blink of an eye. I've never felt something so raw and intense.

He doesn't let up, giving me more as his tongue works over me, fucking me with his skilled fingers. He sucks against my clit, teasing me relentlessly. I need to scream. I need to cry out. I need to fucking come already, but I wouldn't dare. No, I'm holding onto this one as long as I can, even if it kills me.

His tongue is pure magic, whereas his fingers are clearly blessed by the angels of heaven because no man I've ever met has ever had skill like this.

My body spasms wildly out of control, and he uses his other hand to try and hold me still.

"Oh God. YES!" I cry out, every second bringing me closer and closer to the edge. It's too much, I can't handle it, but I'm not going out just yet, and I lean up on one elbow, needing to see the way his fingers slide in and out, desperate to watch the way his wet tongue rolls over my needy clit. And fuck, it's the most erotic thing I've ever seen.

His long, thick fingers separate inside of me, rolling past my walls over and over, driving me wild with need as I become completely captivated by the view. My hips buck beneath his hold, and I feel his wicked grin against my clit. I'm so fucking wet for him, but something tells me this is only the beginning.

I hook my joined wrists around the back of his strong neck, holding on for dear life as he pushes me past my limits, my clit becoming more sensitive by the second. "Oh. Fuck. I can't—I'm . . . Shit. Oh God. Oh God. YES!"

My fingers knot into his hair, and a deep growl rumbles through my bedroom, the vibration against my clit sending me into overdrive. Then without another second of warning, I detonate, coming harder than I've ever come before. My body spasms as the walls of my pussy wildly convulse around his huge fingers.

I cry out as my orgasm tears through me, feeling its effects right into my fingertips and toes. I clench my eyes and throw my head back, never having felt more alive in my life. Not even I could entice an orgasm like this out of me.

Holy fucking shit.

He doesn't stop, and with every swipe of his fingers and tongue against my sensitive body, he drags my orgasm out, and my thighs involuntarily squeeze around his head as my hips wildly buck and shake. It's too much, and I fall back to the mattress as the high threatens to take me out.

"Oh my god," I pant as it finally hits its peak and begins to wind back down.

Mr. Christmas Eve reluctantly gives in and allows me a chance to come down, slowly pulling his fingers free before letting up on my clit and pulling back just enough for my body to relax. He takes my thighs and lifts them off his shoulders before placing my feet back on the edge of the bed.

I can't tear my eyes off him as my chest heaves, only as he gets back to his feet, looming over me in the soft moonlight—all six-foot-four of him—I'm met with his raging erection, and fuck, he's ready to go. Eating my pussy really worked him up, and judging by the protruding veins and the bead of pre-cum sitting on the tip of his massive cock, he's more than ready for me.

He steps into me, his legs hitting the edge of the mattress before his hand comes down beside my hip. He leans over me, hovering just close enough to tease me but not actually touch me. That is until he brings his other hand up and hovers his glistening fingertips over my lips. "Open wide, Mila. Taste how sweet you are."

I open my mouth just enough for him to slide his thick fingers inside, and I close my eyes as I suck them clean. He pulls them free, and before I have the chance to swallow, his lips come down on mine, his tongue sweeping into my mouth and kissing me deeply.

I moan against his lips, and he slowly pulls away, dropping his lips to the sensitive skin below my ear and driving me wild. I tip my head back as I arch up off the bed. "Oh God," I groan, hooking my legs around his hips and pulling him down until I feel his heavy cock grinding against my core.

"Free my wrists," I beg him, panting as his hips grind down.

He reaches up to my bound wrists, and with the quickest flick of his fingers, I'm freed. I don't hesitate to slip my hand between our bodies and wrap my fingers around his base, slowly pumping. "God, I need to fuck you."

He shakes his head. "No, Mila. You're enjoying the ride. Tonight, I fuck you until your legs shake."

A thrill rumbles through my chest, quickly building until it's almost too much to bear, and when he pulls back and rests on his knees between my thighs, the anticipation is enough to paralyze me.

With one tug, my garter belt snaps, and he tosses it aside before taking the delicate material of my thong and slowly dragging it down over my hips and thighs. The sight of me in nothing but a bra and heels makes him pause, and he sinks his teeth into his lower lip as he fists his cock, slowly stroking it. For just a moment, I wonder how the hell that's supposed to fit inside me. But this is a Christmas wish, right? It has to fit. This man, who may or may not be Santa Claus, wouldn't have brought me equipment that's incompatible with my body. That doesn't mean he ever intended to make it easy for me. He's going to make me work for it.

The sensual way he strokes himself is doing wicked things to me, and I squirm in anticipation, my pussy about to come apart from just the thought of what he's about to do to me. Then as if to put me at ease, he scoops his arm beneath my hips and lifts me just enough to line me up with his angry cock. "I hope you're ready for me, Mila."

My tongue rolls along my bottom lip, my eyes hooded and filled with fire. "Do your worst."

And with that, he guides his thick tip straight into my entrance.

I suck in a breath, feeling the instant satisfaction as my walls begin to stretch around him, almost to the point of pain, and judging by the look on his face, I'm not the only one affected by this. He sinks deeper, inch by inch, taking all the time in the world, and when his thumb presses down on my clit and rubs slow circles, my body starts to shake.

This is going to be too much, but I am so down for the ride. Whatever he wants to give me, I'm ready to take.

He keeps going, giving me his full length until he bottoms out, and fuck, I've never been stretched so far in my life. He pauses just a moment, letting me adjust to his sheer size, and when he slowly begins to pull back, my walls finally start to relax around him.

"Holy shit," I groan low.

"Fuck, baby. I'm only just getting started."

He thrusts back inside of me, and as his thumb works my clit, I can't help but reach beneath me and unclasp my bra, desperate to get rid of it. "Shit," I gasp. "Again."

He rolls his hips and hits that desperate spot deep inside of me, fucking me just like I wished. My walls clench around him, squeezing him as tight as I can. It's too much. He's too good.

"That's right, Mila. Take all of me. Just like that."

Oh God. The gravel in his deep tone sends pulses of electricity shooting right through my body and straight to my core, and when he adds just a little more pressure to my clit, I lose all control.

"Hold on to it, baby. Don't you dare come."

Only it's too late, and I detonate again, my pussy shattering like glass around him. "Oh shit," I cry out, clenching my eyes. He doesn't stop, still wildly thrusting deep inside me. Then before I've even reached the height of my orgasm, he flips me over, props me on my knees, and before my pussy has even stopped spasming, he slams back inside me from behind.

"Oh fuck," I groan, burying my face into the blankets as my hands ball into tight fists. I push back against him, taking him deeper as his hand takes my hip, his fingers digging into my flesh.

I come down from my high, but as he keeps fucking me, my body quickly starts working back up again.

With my ass high in the air, his other hand comes down in a firm spank against my skin, and as the sweetest burn stings my ass, he soothes it with a gentle rub of his palm before his fingers trail down to my hole, applying just enough pressure to drive me insane.

"Show me how you please yourself, Mila. Rub your clit."

Without hesitation, I slip my hand between my legs, and the

second my fingers brush my sensitive clit, my hips jolt with need. I grind against my fingers as he slams into my cunt over and over, the rotation of his hips almost too much to bear.

His bulging tip moves inside of me, hitting the spot just the way I like it, and as he pushes his skilled fingers against my ass, teasing me with the sweetest pleasure, I succumb to his wicked ways, and for the fourth time tonight, an intense orgasm rips through my body.

"Fuck," I cry out, barely able to hold myself up a second longer.

He lets me ride it out, but the way his fingers dig into my hip and the way he grunts through his clenched jaw suggests he's just as far out on the edge as I am, and honestly, all he needs is a little push.

Determination floods me, and despite the way I'm currently falling to pieces, I push back against him, taking him harder, deeper, and falling in love with the way he clutches me as though he'll never get enough.

He grunts, and just as I reach the absolute peak of my orgasm, he comes hard, shooting hot spurts of cum deep inside of me.

CHAPTER 6

MILA

My head crashes against my pillow as my not-so-mysterious Christmas Eve stalker comes down beside me, his hand resting against my ass as we each struggle to catch our breath.

"Shit, Mila. I could fuck you every minute of every day for the rest of my life and still not have enough of you."

A stupid grin stretches across my face, and I drop my hand on his chest, feeling the rapid beat of his heart below. "Is that a challenge? Because I think you might have worked out that I'm not the type to shy away from a challenge."

"No, you're certainly not," he agrees.

I can't help but laugh as I simply stare at him. This can't be real.

This man is far too perfect for me, and yet I don't know a damn thing about him. "Are you ready to tell me your name now?"

A cocky smirk pulls at his lips. "I thought you would have put it together by now."

My brows furrow, unsure what he could mean. It's not like I can simply guess his name. All this time, I've been assuming he was Santa Claus, but that couldn't be right because I saw Santa when I was six, and this guy wasn't him. Don't get me wrong, he was certainly there, but he wasn't the old man in red putting presents under my tree.

"Honestly, I don't really know," I admit, pushing up until I'm sitting cross-legged beside him. "From that very first time I saw you when I was a kid, my little brain assumed you were Santa's son, and that's stuck with me all this time."

He nods. "Well, your little kid brain was right. I am his son. Only he's no longer Santa Claus. I am, but I prefer to go by Nick."

My face scrunches. "Santa Claus, huh?" I say slowly, letting it really sink in as a million different thoughts filter through my brain. I mean, how can his father simply not be Santa anymore? But also, is he Nick as in jolly old Saint Nicholas?

Nick sits up against the headboard and lets out a heavy sigh. "Okay, then. Hit me with it. I know you have questions."

"If you are Santa, what the hell are you doing here with me? Don't you have like . . . I don't know, a billion gifts to deliver to kids all over the world?"

"Two and a half billion," he corrects. "And no, I'm all done for the night. You'd be surprised just how quickly I can get my job done when I know there's a beautiful woman here waiting for me to fuck her into oblivion."

A stupid smile pulls across my lips as I feel my cheeks begin to flush. "Okay, so you've made all the children of the world happy, but how did you do it? Is the whole reindeer and sleigh thing real?"

He nods and points toward the ceiling. "They're waiting up on the roof."

My eyes bug out of my head. "Holy fucking shit. You're lying. There's magical reindeer on the roof right now?"

Nick laughs. "Yes. They can be dicks sometimes, but after the night they've had, they're pretty chill right now. You could come up and meet them if you'd like."

"Really? Would that be okay?"

"Of course."

I bite down on my lip, feeling a swell of butterflies deep in my stomach, knowing if I'm not careful, I could so easily fall in love with this man, which is so stupidly ridiculous considering I will only ever see him once a year. Assuming he wakes me up of course.

"So, how come you're Santa now? You don't exactly look like a typical Santa."

Nick laughs. "Believe me, I know," he says. "It's a bit of a sore point with my old man back home. But being Santa is a family thing. Passed down from father to son for generations, and a few years back, my father—the Santa of your childhood—retired and passed the reins to me."

"So, you're it now."

"Yep."

"Shit. No pressure, huh?"

"You've got no fucking idea," he murmurs before setting his gaze on me, a heaviness beginning to settle between us as I realize it's almost time for him to leave.

"You have to go, don't you?"

Nick nods. "Yes, I've completed your wishes and the type of magic I have to do that won't allow me to abuse that power."

"Damn," I sigh. "Does it make a difference if I don't want you to go?"

"I wish it could."

Willing myself not to break, I crawl across my bed and right into his lap, straddling him as he holds my stare. "When you say you've completed all my wishes, does that mean you heard what I said in the fountain?"

He smiles. "Not only did I hear you," he says, digging into his pocket and pulling out a piece of paper. "I also got a printout to make sure I didn't miss anything."

"No way," I laugh, taking the piece of paper and glancing over the exact wishes I had made with Carolina while shivering outside of the fountain, my teeth chattering from the cold.

☐ *I wish to be dicked down so hard that my knees will shake for weeks after.*

☐ *I wish to be thrown around, flipped over like a pancake and railed within an inch of my life.*

☐ *I wish to be dragged down my bed only to feel a warm mouth close over my clit and scream as he works me with his skilled tongue.*

☐ *I wish to make him come apart in my mouth.*

☐ *I wish to come alive, to feel things I've never felt before, and to be screwed so good that nothing will ever compare.*

"Oh my god. This is so embarrassing," I say, covering my face. "And yet, I can't bring myself to regret it."

"Even if I told you my old man saw these too?"

My face drains of color, and I gape at him in horror, my heart racing as humiliation washes over me. "Please tell me you're lying."

"Really wish I could," he tells me, not bothering to spare my feelings for even a second, though he doesn't strike me as the type to play silly games. He'll give it to me straight. "So, tell me, Mila. Have I completed your wishes to your satisfaction?"

"Ooh, I don't know," I tease, reaching across to my bedside table and pulling out the top drawer to fetch a pen, my gaze momentarily lingering on my charm bracelet and getting butterflies at the thought of this man being responsible for that. Sitting up straight, I hold up the list and drop my gaze. "Let's see, shall we?"

Nick rolls his eyes. "Did I dick you down so good your legs shook?"

I grin, not bothering to be shy about it, especially after what he just did to me. "Yes."

He nods to the paper. "Tick it."

☐ *I wish to be dicked down so hard that my knees will shake for weeks after.*

"Good girl," he murmurs, watching as I confidently tick off my first wish. "Now, did I flip you over like a pancake and rail you within an inch of your life?"

I smile again, remembering it so damn clearly that my pussy clenches. "You certainly did."

"Good. Tick it."

I get back to work, clutching the pen as I tick the second box.

☐ *I wish to be thrown around, flipped over like a pancake and railed within an inch of my life.*

Glancing back up and waiting for him to continue, I realize he hasn't glanced down at the paper once. It's as though he has every last one of my filthy Christmas wishes completely memorized, which only has my heart racing just a little faster.

"What about that sweet little clit of yours?" he questions, his hand falling to my hip and gently squeezing, making my skin burn with electricity from his touch. "Did you feel my mouth and how I worked you with my tongue? Did I make you scream, Mila?"

"Oh God, yes," I groan.

"Mark it off."

☐ *I wish to be dragged down my bed only to feel a warm mouth close over my clit and scream as he works me with his skilled tongue.*

"Now," he continues in that deep, gravelly tone, leaning in so his lips are gently brushing across my ear. "We both know damn well how you made me come apart in your mouth, so go right ahead and tick that one off. But the real question is, have you felt things tonight that you've never felt before? Did I screw you so good that no other man will ever compare to how it was with me?"

I suck in a breath, my body so responsive to everything that he is.

I don't get a chance to respond before his arms are around my waist and he rolls us until he's hovering over me, his body heavy against mine, but not so heavy that he crushes me. "Tell me, Mila. Will any other man ever compare to this?"

"Never," I say just as he slides that thick cock back inside of me, slowly rocking back and forth as his lips come down on mine, and at this point, I don't even know where the list or the pen have gone. All that matters is how he feels inside of me.

It's slow and sensual, almost like some kind of beautiful goodbye.

I hold on to him as he brings me to the edge and it's not long before we're coming together again, and considering that wasn't one of my wishes, I can only guess that it was nothing more than a gift from him to me.

His lips come down on mine with a heaviness that tears me to shreds. He sighs. "I'm sorry, Mila. I have to go."

I slowly nod, willing myself not to break as I clutch his hand in mine. "Is it still okay that I walk up to the roof?"

"Of course."

A renewed excitement builds deep in my chest, realizing that I still have a few minutes to hold onto this insane fantasy—a fantasy not a single person across the globe will ever believe.

Nick climbs off my bed, pulling me up with him, and as he finds his clothes and starts to dress, all I can do is grab my silk dressing gown and watch, still unable to believe tonight is even real. After kicking off my heels and switching them out for a pair of slippers, I pull the gown tight around me, tying it in a knot at my waist.

Nick fixes his pants and steps into his boots before grabbing his big red coat off my armchair and pulling it on. Only he doesn't bother doing it up or strapping his belt back on. Instead, he simply wraps it around his hand and leads me out of my bedroom.

We cross the living room and before I know it, Nick is taking my hand and helping me through my fire escape. "You know," I say as he climbs out behind me, then makes sure to close the window to keep the chill from getting in. "Every year since I was a little girl, I wished you would come back."

"I know," he says, starting up the stairs toward his reindeer, who are no doubt waiting as patiently as ever. "I received every single one of them."

"You never let me down," I muse. "You came every year."

"Wouldn't miss it for the world, Mila," he says, stopping on the stairs and stepping right into me, crowding me against the railing. "I've belonged to you since I was eight years old. There wasn't a single year I didn't want to come. Even if you never wished me back, I would have found my way here."

My heart races, but I really don't know how to feel. He's leaving me, and I'm just supposed to wait for him to return. My heart is so full, but at the same time, it's breaking in a way I never thought capable. "So," I say, trying to deflect the pain growing in my chest. "Are you a creepy, stalker Santa who likes getting his rocks off, or are you a genuine man who simply wanted a girl's Christmas wishes to come true?"

Nick grins and lets his hand fall into mine as we continue up the next flight of stairs. "Two things can be true at the same time."

"Wait. What do you mean? Just how much stalking are we talking about?"

"Don't ask questions you don't want answers to, Mila."

I swallow hard, wondering just what kind of man he is. Is he truly stalking me? Does he come to see me more than I know, or is it much more sinister than that? One thing I know for sure is that he's right. I shouldn't ask questions I don't want to know the answers to.

I'm happy living in my little delusional bubble, assuming he's some kind of white knight who's going to show up every Christmas Eve and make all my wild Christmas fantasies come true.

"So, you're all about the whole spreading joy thing, I take it?"

"No," he laughs. "My old man is all about spreading joy. Me? I prefer to spread legs."

Holy fuck.

A shiver sails down my spine, as a strange need pulses through my core. How could I possibly be ready for more after the fuck fest he just put me through? "Yeah," I say. "And you certainly do it well."

Nick laughs, and as we near the roof, he glances down at me, his eyes sparkling brighter than the stars in the sky. "You know the song 'I Saw Mommy Kissing Santa Claus'?" he questions.

My brows furrow wondering where the hell he's going with this. "Yeah," I say slowly. "Isn't that the one where the kid sees his mom with Santa, only we all knew it was just his dad?"

Nick shakes his head. "Uhhhh . . . maybe I shouldn't have brought this up."

"What the hell are you talking about, Nicholas Claus? Wait. Is that your last name? Or is it Kringle? Like Kris Kringle?"

"It's just Saint Nicholas. No last name. But don't be calling me Saint Nicholas, that's my father. I just go by Nick."

"Okay, Nick. Tell me the kid in that song wasn't actually seeing you kiss his mom."

Nick laughs as his smirk widens. "Guilty," he says. "Only, I wasn't kissing her, I was fu—"

"HOLY FUCKING SHIT," I screech, cutting him off. "That's one of my favorite Christmas songs, and now I can never sing it again."

"I'm kidding," he chuckles. "That song's been around for years. It was actually my grandfather who was caught getting his dick wet."

"Ewwww." I go to reprimand him further when my eyes widen in horror. "Wait. Does that mean I'm not your first Christmas Eve screw while on the job?"

His eyes widen just a fraction before quickly recovering. "Might I remind you that you've had a boyfriend for the past however many years. Did you expect me to hold out all these years waiting for you to realize just how much of a filthy girl you are for me?"

I shrug. He kind of has a point.

"And just so you know," Nick continues. "Creeping into your room in the middle of the night is hardly as much fun when there's another man in your bed," he tells me. "Where is he, by the way? Did you finally drop the dead weight?"

"The dead weight had an issue keeping his dick in his pants."

"Oh shit. Sorry I brought it up."

I shrug my shoulders. "You know, it's been really bothering me these past few weeks since it happened, but after tonight, I don't seem to care anymore."

Nick holds my stare for just a moment, and I can feel the weight of all the things unsaid between us. Just as I try to figure out a way to explain the million different things rushing through my mind, we reach the roof, and my whole world explodes into a million pieces.

"What in the ever-loving fuck?" I mutter to myself, pausing on the top step as I see the big red sleigh surrounded by eight sleeping reindeer. My brain can barely process it, but it's right there in front of me. Every Christmas story told to me as a child suddenly flashes in my mind, and I can't help but gape at the sight.

"Which one of them is Rudolph?" I ask, keeping my voice down so as not to wake them.

Nick tugs my hand, bringing me closer to his . . . pets? Or are they employees? I suppose I don't really know. "Reindeer only have a lifespan of fifteen to eighteen years. The original reindeer you would know from all those famous stories and songs are long gone. These are their descendants. There's been generations of reindeer since the original ones."

"Oh," I say, feeling slightly disappointed, but I suppose it makes sense.

"This one though," he says, striding up to the one sleeping closest to us before bending down and gently brushing his fingers between its eyes. "This is Tucker. He's a direct descendant of Dasher and Comet."

"Wait. Dasher and Comet had babies together? I thought all the reindeer were female."

"No," he says. "They have to reproduce somehow. But Dasher and Comet, theirs was a love story for the ages."

A stupid smile pulls across my face, and I watch as Nick

straightens up to his full height and makes his way back toward me, the heaviness in his eyes killing me.

This is it. He has to go. And then what?

My heart breaks as he steps back into me, and as if reading my mind, he takes my hand and pulls me into his wide chest. "Wish me back, Mila. As long as you wish for me, I will continue to come."

I nod. Twelve whole months until I get to see him again.

His lips drop to mine, and he kisses me with such sincerity that every piece of my broken heart mends back together. Only when he pulls away, I feel myself falling apart again. His forehead drops to mine, and he almost looks pained. I can't help but wonder if being here for so long is somehow physically affecting him.

His hand falls away from my waist and he digs into his pocket before pulling out a single silver charm and placing it into my hand. Looking down, I can't help but smile as I take in the little charm. It's the Naughty List with my name scrawled right in the center.

"It's perfect," I whisper.

Nick nods and squeezes my hand, and with that, he turns away, heading right for his sleigh as the eight reindeer suddenly wake, looking as though they have all the energy in the world.

Then in a blink of an eye, they're gone, leaving the roof as empty as my heart.

I clutch the Naughty List charm as the tears begin to well in my eyes, and when the chill in the air becomes too much to tolerate, I hurry back down the fire escape and into my apartment. Making my way back into my bedroom, I collapse onto my bed before taking the charm bracelet on my bedside table and hastily adding this one to the string of others, putting it right at the front. This particular one will always hold so much more value to me than the others.

The tears don't stop flowing, and as I roll over, I feel something in my bed. Feeling around the sheets, I find the red satin cloth he used to bind my wrists, the pen, and the printout of my Christmas wishes.

Taking the pen, I hold up the list and glance over the final wish before finally ticking it, knowing without a single doubt that no other man will ever compare to the night I just had with Nick. No other man will ever make me feel so alive, and no other man will ever make me feel the way he did.

☐ *I wish to come alive, to feel things I've never felt before, and to be screwed so good that nothing will ever compare.*

CHAPTER 7

MILA

JANUARY

Making my way down the busy New York street, I stop at the very fountain Carolina pulled me into only a few short weeks ago. Only now the slushie fountain is rock-hard ice. If I didn't want to risk looking like a moron, I could probably put on a pair of ice skates and whip around on it.

Parking my ass on the edge of the fountain, I pull out the little letter I've written a million times over these past few weeks, not really sure what I'm supposed to be doing with this whole wish thing.

In the past, I've just closed my eyes and wished. It didn't matter where I was or how it happened. All I know is that I made the wish inside my head and come Christmas morning, the little charm for my bracelet would appear. Only now it feels different. A simple wish almost doesn't seem enough after the night we spent together.

But what really confuses me is what I am supposed to wish for.

The raunchy wish I'd made was done after drinking two bottles of cheap wine, and now that I know that I can ask him for just about anything in the world, my options are endless. Figuring out what to wish for though . . . that is a struggle.

But also, are Christmas wishes made in January still valid? I don't know what kind of magic it is that allows him to be able to whip around the whole globe in a single night and visit over two billion homes, but does that magic extend outside of the Christmas season?

I've got no fucking clue, and sitting here on the edge of a frozen fountain with my letter to Santa makes me feel like such a fucking loser. If anybody were to stop and ask what I was doing, they'd have me committed and strapped to a bed in a straitjacket.

Shaking off the doubt, my gaze trails down to the letter as I unfold it, reading over it one last time and hoping that I get this right.

Dear Nick, A.K.A the PussySlayer3000,

I have no idea what I'm doing, but what I do know is that my boring wishes of the past are going to stay in the past. After discovering just what you and your big red sleigh are capable of, I feel it's time we start pushing some boundaries.

There are twelve months in the year, and considering the five checkbox wishes you so graciously allowed me to make this past Christmas, I'm going to go ahead and assume having twelve wishes really isn't too much to ask. Though, I was thoroughly exhausted after your last visit. I don't know if my lady taco can physically handle any more than five wishes, but as we recently discovered, I'm more than up for a good challenge.

By the way, you completely rocked my world in case you hadn't realized. I just hate that you had to leave, but I get it.

So, here's the deal. Every month, I'm going to come and sit right here on the edge of this stupid fountain and send you my wish. As for the letter, I have no idea if you're actually going to get it or if all of this is going to be some big waste of time. But I'm committed now.

There's no going back.

Anyway, for my first wish this Christmas, I think it comes as no surprise that I need you to take me the second you see me. It's going to be a looooong year waiting for you to appear in my stupidly cramped living room, so we're going to need a quickie just to get it out of our systems. After that, we can take our time! Might I suggest throwing me up against the wall and slamming inside of me? Don't worry, I'll be ready for you this year. No accidentally falling asleep this time.

Anyway, that's it. I don't really know what else I'm supposed to say, only that I kinda miss you. Is that ridiculous?

Love always,
Your Christmess Eve Stalker.

I'm not exactly thrilled with my letter, but honestly, I have no idea what I'm supposed to say to the guy who's been stalking me for the past twenty years. He thoroughly rocked my world, and if I'm completely honest, it took well over three days before I was able to walk around without feeling exactly where he'd been. I loved every second of it.

Christmas morning came, and I didn't even notice how alone I was. All I could think about was the night I'd just spent with a man who I think is amazing. Truth be told, I guess I don't really know. He's the perfect stranger, and yet, I feel like my soul instantly knew him. That's weird, right?

Fuck.

Feeling the chill of the late January air, I stand from the fountain's edge and turn to look at what's usually flowing water. My plan was to toss the letter into the water, just like I'd tossed the penny in, but I suppose that's not going to work today considering it's completely frozen over.

Trying to figure out a plan, I shamelessly search around the fountain, probably looking like a fucking idiot, before finally finding a loose tile along the fountain edge and lifting it up. Sliding the Christmas letter wish beneath it, I let out a heavy breath, and deciding there's no going back now, I lower the tile back down and walk away, hoping like hell he receives it.

<u>FEBRUARY</u>

To the Midnight Pussy Penetrator with Exceptional Tongue Game,

Sooo . . . I wasn't going to tell you this, but I lied in my last letter.

I don't just kinda miss you. I miss you a lot, which I feel really stupid about. I didn't realize I could become so attached to someone after only one night. But then, is it only just one night? It's more like 20 years of thinking about you. Wondering who you are and what kind of man you became. (By the way, I really appreciate the kind of man you've grown into. Like really, really appreciate it.)

It's been two months since Christmas, and I still haven't figured out how to write a proper letter to you. I'm still stuck on what to say. Hell, I don't even know if you're getting these or not, but like I said in my last letter, I'm committed now. I'm seeing this through right until I get to see you again.

So, here I go, for my second wish, Mr. Genie, I need you to keep exploring my small apartment. By this point, we would have already screwed up against the wall, but I feel as though the kitchen counter is missing out. So, why don't we head over there and give the walls of the kitchen something to talk about? I've been thinking about that skilled tongue of yours a lot, so let's put it back into action. Spread my thighs and go to town with that mouth. Make my whole body crumble, but also, be creative about it. I want to feel as though I'm the most desirable woman in the world.

Love Always,
Santa's Favorite Ho!

<u>MARCH</u>

To the Dick-Me-Down Demon,

We're three months into the year and I'm already going crazy. To put it bluntly, I'm horny as all hell! What are the chances of an accidental pre-Christmas sacrificial fucking? I know it's against the rules and all that, and I'm sure granting Christmas wishes outside of the giving season is frowned upon, but damn. I have an itch and it desperately needs to be scratched.

How am I supposed to last till the end of the year? I've run my batteries dead on every single one of my vibrators, but despite how I loved my vibrators before, they're not even getting the job done. You ruined me for everything else. Though I suppose that's on me. I wished for you to fuck me so good that nothing else could ever compare. I didn't realize just how literally you'd take that.

Orgasms aren't even fun now. I just need to come so hard that I feel the earth shake beneath my feet . . . . or back, assuming you'll have me on my back when you make that happen.

That's my wish by the way. All I need is to come so damn hard my world implodes.

Please and thank you.

Love always,

A Girl Whose Fingers Are Sore from Frantically Trying to Get Off and Failing.

APRIL

To my Dearest Saint Nicholas, (but not your dad because that would be weird!!)

I've been doing some thinking, and I think I've fucked up. I've gone too hard in my first three wishes. I won't be able to survive the night, especially if we go in order. So from here on out, I need to be careful. I need to make sure we can make it right through to the final wish, otherwise, I won't just be disappointed in myself, I'll be devastated.

What's the point of getting to have all these wishes if I can't actually have them?

In other news, my bosses at work are being assholes, and it's really making for a shit time. Kinda hating the thought of getting up every morning and slaving away for them. I don't really have much else going on at the moment.

My whole life feels like it's in shambles. My ex finally realized how badly he fucked up and came crawling back, and after I told him to get lost, he tried to get in my pants. But not even my desperation to be railed will have me welcoming him back into my bed.

As for the whole friend situation, Carolina finally got the promotion she'd been working for, but now she's one of my bosses and pretends as though we were never friends, and as for my ex-bestie, I still can't find it in me to forgive her. I don't think I ever will.

Maybe I'm just feeling weird this month because it would have been my father's sixtieth birthday.

I suppose for my wish this month, I just want to be able to feel something. I'll leave that one up to you to figure out.

Love always,
Mila
xxx

MAY

To the One and Only Clitermas Extraordinaire,

Okay sooooooo . . . My last letter was a bit of a buzz kill. Bet you got real hard over that shit.

I would like to tell you that everything has gotten a bit better and that I stuck it to my bosses, but surprise, surprise, I haven't. I bitched out.

But in other news, at least I don't feel quite so pathetic.

I've been using all my spare time to try and come up with a solution to my lack of getting off situation, and I feel I've come up with something that could potentially do the trick. So for my next Christmas wish (I'm starting to lose count. How many are we up to? Is this number five or six?) I wish to have a perfect mold of your dick that I can ride anytime I want. This way, whenever the mood strikes, I won't be shamefully let down by my own inability to get the job done. (Must come with veins and all. Batteries not included! Also, Christmas red is suddenly my new favorite color, so let's roll with that!)

Love always,
Your Magical Christmas Cum Dumpster

<u>JUNE</u>

To Nicholas (no last name), the Heavyweight Girth Champion,

I don't even know if you're getting these letters. I've been leaving them at the same fountain I made my wish last year and they're all still here, so I'm assuming you get copies? How does that even work? There are so many questions! I found a loose tile, and so far it's been doing well to conceal all of my letters, but it's getting a little crowded in there.

On to the important things. My wish.

So, last month I wished for a huge replica of your cock to ride, and the moment I sent my wish off into the universe (beneath the broken tile) I was insanely jealous. Why am I out here riding a replica of your massive appendage when I haven't even gotten a chance to ride the real one? So that's my wish this month. I'm going to ride you as I see fit. On the floor. On the couch. On the rooftop beside your sleeping reindeer. I haven't quite worked it out. But what I do know is that you're going to lay back and take everything I'm willing to give you. And boy, I better see you fall apart.

Yours truly,

The Sexual Deviant Who's Going to Bring You to Your Knees

<u>JULY</u>

To the Dick-Tator of My Wettest Dreams,

Call me sentimental, but we're past the six-month mark, and I won't lie, this year is turning out harder than I thought, and I'm missing you more than you could know. This Christmas, I just want to know more about you. I want more time with you. I just need . . . more.

Seeing you disappear into thin air and waiting for something I don't know will ever come has killed me. I can't lie to you, Nick. I think my heart broke when you left.

So that's all I'm wishing for this month, just to get to know you better. To know the real you. I don't want you to hold anything back.

I'm sorry, you were probably hoping for some raunchy wish to come through so you could spend the rest of the month jerking off to my words. My bad. I promise, I'll do better next month. I hope.

Maybe it's my fault. I've alienated myself from the world, I still hate my job, and I have no friends. I can't talk to anybody about you. Hell, I'm starting to wonder if my mom was right all those years ago. Are you just a figment of my imagination? Was last Christmas nothing more than a wild dream?

Sorry.

Yours always,
A Girl Terrified of Breaking Her Own Heart

<u>AUGUST</u>

To My Dearest Master Baitor,

Okay. I know you said something about being a creepy Santa Stalker, but just how far does that go? Have you been checking in on me, or are these letters enough to keep your raging erection at bay? I suppose life has been hard. (Just as I assume you've been all year.)

Tell me, Santa, do you still picture me from that night? Think about the way you spread me apart and ravaged me? I do. Every moment of every day. I hardly get anything done.

I don't know how much longer I can wait. Not getting to be with you right now is killing me. Not to mention, at this point, I'm pretty sure I'm writing these letters to a figment of my imagination. I might need to see somebody about this.

But what I really need is to feel you sliding into me from behind. I want you to bend me over, wrap your hand around my hair and fuck me from behind. I want it rough. Don't you dare hold back. And when you're done, I need you to tell me what a good girl I was.

I want you in my mouth while I ride your replica cock. I want it all.

Fuck, I'm too horny for my own good.

There you have it, my raunchiest of Santas. That's my filthy Christmas wish.

P.S. Happy jerking!

P.P.S. I wouldn't be opposed to handcuffs or blindfolds.

Yours truly,

A Woman Wondering If Her Saucy Santa Might Be Down for a Bit of Ass Play

SEPTEMBER

To the Pining Pussy Perpetrator,

I've been thinking more about this whole ass-play thing. I'm curious. I'm not quite sure if it's a wish at this point, but can we not wipe it completely off the table just yet?

Let's play around, see how I feel. It's already going to be such a big night, and to be honest, I've not exactly had the greatest sexual partners in the past who've made me feel very comfortable in that situation. So, let's pencil it into the roster. Santa is going to possibly claim my ass.

Buuuuuut . . . . maybe I should prepare myself a bit. After all, the sheer size of your cock would probably tear me in half, and I know I say I'm always up for a challenge, but some challenges simply take it too far.

Can we count this as a half wish, like a possibility wish?

Please and thank you.

Though, in the meantime, just know that I'm all the way over here in New

York in my tiny piece-of-shit apartment, spending my free time preparing my ass for your possible invasion. Don't worry, I'll be careful and start slow. There will be plenty of lube all over my body, and as I touch and stretch myself, it'll be you I'm thinking of.

I do hope that gives you a nice visual to work with.

Always,
Your Dick Demoness

OCTOBER

To the Beastly Bitch Banger,

I finally did it. I quit my job, and I don't really know where to go from here.

I'm not exactly struggling. I have plenty of inheritance from my father's estate, but like . . . what am I even doing? I'm taking up space in this shitty little apartment that doesn't offer me any kind of life and about to start looking for jobs just as terrible as the one I left.

What is this life? Surely there must be something better for me in the grand scheme of things.

I wish I could be with you all the time. I don't even know where you live or what you do with the other three hundred and sixty-four days of the year, but I'm sure you have it better than I do.

Ugh! Look at me ranting when I should be using this time to write you an exciting letter, though it doesn't look like this one is shaping up to be very much fun.

I suppose I'm missing you.

Fuck. That's a lie. I more than miss you. I think I'm getting too attached to the idea of you. I think I might even be falling for you.

Anyway, for my wish this month, I'm not really sure. I mean, if you consider all the other wishes, I really don't know what kind of energy we'll have left. Though, you don't strike me as the type to give up from a lack of energy. You're the power through type. And in that case, my wish is for you to surprise me.

Give or do something I'm not expecting.

Yours always,
The Radiant Little Ray of Fuckable Sunshine

<u>NOVEMBER</u>

To He Who I Assume Has the Bluest of Balls Right About Now,

I'm sorry. I don't know what I'm doing. Maybe I'm having second thoughts about all of this. I've been sitting around writing letters to a man I'll never truly be able to have, and what's worse is I think I'm well and truly in love with you. I'm such an idiot.

I suppose my wish for this letter is to have some clarity. I want to see you so bad, but at what point do I move on with my life? Do I spend the rest of my life sitting by this stupid fountain and shoving little love letters under a tile, or do I move on and try to find somebody to settle down with? Maybe get a big house and pop out a few kids just like my father always wanted for me.

I keep finding myself wondering about what a life with you might look like, and I'm sure that's absurd, right? You're Santa Claus for fuck's sake. What am I to you? Just some girl you get to fuck come Christmas. Where's Mrs. Claus? Are you married with a bunch of little elf-like children running around?

Fuck. Maybe I'm wasting my time with all of this.

Don't get me wrong, I'm really excited to see you. I suppose I'm just conflicted.

At what point am I supposed to grow up and make something of myself, you know?

Anyway, I've started putting Christmas decorations up early, trying to get into the Christmas spirit and all that crap. Halloween is well and truly over and now the whole world is focused solely on you.

Kinda jealous of all the attention you're getting from all these other women. Though to be fair, they think you're nothing more than a myth. If only they knew just how well that myth got me off last year.

I'm counting down the days until I get to see you.

Love always,
Your Mila

DECEMBER

To the Christmas Cunt-Stable with the Big Jingle Balls,

Okay. Christmas is well and truly here, and despite not accepting any of the ridiculous job offers and being the loneliest person in the world, I'm allowing myself to be excited, even if Christmas doesn't feel like Christmas anymore. To be fair, I don't think that has anything to do with you. Seeing you is the only thing really keeping me from falling apart.

I bought a little something for you, and despite losing count of how many actual wishes I've made, my final one is to watch you tear it off me with your teeth.

God, I really can't wait. I have butterflies just thinking about what our night will be like.

I hope I haven't scared you away by admitting that I was falling head over heels in love with you. I still think it's ridiculous to love somebody I hardly know, but there's no doubt about it. It's there and as real as it could ever be.

Today is the twentieth of December. There's only a handful of days until I get to see you, and—ahhh shit. I got all emotional, and now I'm tearing up.

Just hurry, okay? Not getting to see you, feel you, taste you, or have you has almost broken me. I really don't know how I'm supposed to handle it next year.

Truly yours,
Future Mrs. Claus (in my dreams)

Shit. That was too much, wasn't it? But I wrote it in pen, and I really don't want to start over. Just pretend it isn't there. I'll sign off again.

Always,
Your Favorite Little Cream Pie

Always,
Your Favorite Little Cream Pie

91

CHAPTER 8

NICK

Reading over the words of Mila's final letter, I let out a heavy sigh. I've had one hell of a rough year being away from her, but from the sound of it, her year has been complete hell, and despite the cheery words and the comical way she addresses each letter, I sense the pain within her.

She's struggling, and I fucking hate that I can't fix it. She's lonely and miserable, and I'm the one person she needs to take that ache away, but I'm the only fucking person on this godforsaken earth who can't be with her.

Fuck. I'd give anything to keep her. To take her away from that bullshit apartment in New York and have her as my own for the rest of time. But how can I just tear her away from her life? Don't get me wrong, I've more than thought about it, especially come October when she wished to be with me all the time.

The sinister thoughts pounding through my mind are enough to see me jailed. She doesn't truly mean it. She doesn't understand what she's asking for. Like in September when she wished for me to claim her sweet ass. Again, I'll do it without a moment of hesitation, but I really don't think she fully understands what she's getting herself into.

Putting her letter down on top of the other eleven, I lean back in my chair and prop my boots up on the expensive mahogany desk, grateful that I don't have to wait much longer before finally getting to be with her.

Tonight is Christmas Eve, and it's only a few short hours before I take off with Tucker leading my sleigh. We'll get the whole gift-giving part of the night over and done with, and before I know it, I'll be sneaking through Mila's living room window and ticking off every last box.

The thought has my attention shifting to the new printout of Mila's wishes, and my lips pull into a smirk. I had to collate them all, taking out just the wishes within each letter. And fuck, we're up for a big night. I hope she's both mentally and physically prepared.

☐ *January – To be fucked up against the living room wall the second I see her. Slam into her. (A quickie to get it out of our systems.)*

☐ *February – Head over to the kitchen counter and give the walls something* to talk about! (More specifically, fuck her with my tongue.) Spread her creamy thighs and go to town with my mouth. Show her how fucking great it can be.

☐ March – Make her come so hard that her whole world implodes. She wants to feel the whole world shake beneath her, but even I have limits on what my magic can do.

☐ April – Make her feel something. Can be creative with this. And no, she doesn't mean with my cock. She wants her heart to come alive.

☐ May – A perfect mold of my veiny dick, preferably in bright Christmas red. Don't forget the veins! Batteries not included.

☐ June – Let her ride me until I fall apart. I have no choice but to lay back and take it. Floor, couch, or rooftop beside the reindeer. (Preferably not the rooftop. Tucker's a horny little reindeer. I don't need him bricking up while watching my girl fuck me.)

☐ July – Get to know me better. Open up. Let her know the man that I am. Let her understand me and feel the person she's been waiting for isn't going to break her heart.

☐ August – Bend her over and take her from behind, hand in her hair, and don't dare hold back. Be rough with her. Then let her ride the replica cock while I fuck her mouth.

☐ September – Claim that sweet ass if she's up for it. Take it slow. She's new at this.

☐ October – Be with me forever. Going to need clarification on this one.

☐ October – Surprise her. Give her something she's not expecting. One pearl necklace coming right up.

☐ *November - Give her the clarity she deserves.*
☐ *December - Lay her down and tear her lingerie off with my teeth.*

Now, I won't lie, I'm particularly fond of June and September. The idea of laying back and watching her take control has excited me to no end. Just the thought of Mila on top of me and riding my cock as she pleases is getting me hard. Fuck, she's going to be so damn beautiful riding me. The way her body will roll. How she'll grind and groan. I can't fucking wait. But claiming her ass? Fuck. She has no idea how many times I've thought about claiming her sweet ass over the years.

As for the list in general. I don't think we can tick them off in order. I'm going to have to be strategic about the way I start ticking shit off, but that's okay. Something tells me that Mila won't mind what order they come in, as long as she gets everything she wants. And fuck, I'm not about to let her down.

She's been waiting a long fucking time for tonight, and I'm going to do everything in my power to ensure she gets every last thing she has asked for. No matter how long it takes.

Leaving her there on that rooftop last year was a fucking punch to the stomach, and the thought of having to do it again just doesn't sit right with me, but what am I supposed to do? Kidnap her and bring her back here? After all, that's exactly what she wished for, right? She wants to be with me forever, and it's not as though I can do what I need to do in New York. I need to be here at the North

Pole, and if she intends to be with me, then she's going to have to be here with me too.

Fuck. Am I seriously considering this? She'll be pissed. It's one thing to give her what she wants, but I know damn well she didn't understand what she was asking for. It works for me though, and it's not like she's exactly loving her life in New York right now. I could offer her a whole world she's never imagined. Sure, she might be pissed for a little while, but she'll get over it eventually.

Shit. It's barely an hour before I'm due to take off for the night to be the perfect Santa Claus for billions of children, and I'm thinking about kidnapping a woman out of her home. The fuck is wrong with me?

A soft knock sounds at my office door, and I barely have a moment to grab the checklist of Mila's wishes and shove it deep into my pocket before my father strides through the door with a stack of papers in his hand, not bothering to wait for an invitation.

"I think it's about time you and I had a conversation," he says in that gruff tone that suggests I'm about to have my ass handed to me.

My boot falls from the desk, and I sit up, my gaze flashing toward the clock on the edge of my desk. "Uhhhh, can it wait until the morning? Now really isn't the best time. I need to start checking on the reindeer."

"No, Nicholas," he says, dropping the papers down in front of me, only for me to realize these are copies of Mila's letters. "We're going to talk now."

Fuck.

He reaches for one of the letters. "To the Midnight Pussy Penetrator with exceptional tongue game," he starts to read out before pinching a few more. "To the Dick Me Down Demon. The Pussy Perpetrator. The Beastly Bitch Banger."

I cringe, but I can't help the laughter that creeps into my tone. The Beastly Bitch Banger was definitely a favorite of mine. "You saw all of them, huh?"

"No, son. I didn't see them. Frederick did," he snaps. "He almost had a heart attack when he discovered these this morning. I've had to go send him to lie down. You know our helpers are innocent of heart. They can't be seeing filthy letters from your girlfriend in New York. The magic of Christmas comes from the innocence of belief, and these letters put that innocence into question and our whole enterprise at risk."

Hmmm. Girlfriend.

Tell me why I like that so much.

"Shit, Dad. I'm sorry," I say, getting to my feet and grabbing my red coat before pulling it on. "I know these letters have definitely been pushing the boundaries of what we do here. I thought I was catching them all before anyone else saw them. Seems I forgot about the backup drive. I'll apologize to Frederick, but I don't really know what more you want from me. Mila is a grown-ass woman. I can't control her Christmas wishes any more than you can. You know just as well as I do that her wishes are her desires, and the only thing I can do about that is to grant those wishes."

My father gapes at me. "It's Christmas Eve. You can't seriously be thinking of entertaining this . . . this filth."

"Sorry, Pops. It's my call. I'm Santa Claus now. I was able to spend time with her last year and get my job done. I don't see why I can't do it again this season."

My old man simply stares at me in horror, and I can only imagine the million thoughts running through his mind. He regrets retiring because he thinks I'm going to fuck this up, but at some point, he's going to have to learn to trust me.

"Dad," I say, stepping around my desk. "I truly am sorry for the letters. I'll do better to keep that shit to myself in the future, but I won't apologize for anything else. I love her, Dad. I've loved her since I was eight years old, and now that she finally knows who I am, I'm not about to turn my back on her. She's waited twelve long months to see me, and you bet your ass that the moment the last present is delivered, I'll be right there on her rooftop, rushing to see her."

Dad watches me for a moment, his gaze softening. "You're really in love with this woman? This isn't just some filthy need to get your rocks off with some random girl and get under my skin."

"No, Pops. Getting under your skin is just an added bonus."

He lets out a heavy sigh, and I watch as his walls slowly fall down. "Alright then. See to it that you talk to Frederick, and remember, the job comes first. No child is left without a gift before you go see her."

"I know."

"Good," he says, before turning his back and striding to the door, only to stop and glance back. "Oh, and Nick. Keep your filthy sexcapades out of the Christmas wishes. Find another way to communicate with this girl that doesn't traumatize our helpers."

I nod. He has a point. "Noted."

And with that, he's gone, leaving me to prepare for the biggest night of the year. Only this year, everything is going to be different.

CHAPTER 9

MILA

The revealing black lingerie fits better than anything I've ever worn, and as I tie a big red bow around my waist, I can't help but feel like the most desirable woman in the world.

God, I can't wait for him to arrive. It's going to be perfect, even better than last year because, this time, I've spent every day of the last year anticipating his return, trying to remember what he smelled like, how big he was, how demanding. Just the memory of his deep voice gives me chills.

Every day I've thought about him, and despite how badly it's going to hurt to have to see him leave again, I can't help but need this. I've struggled this year. I've had no one in my corner. No family. No friends. It's just been me and my wishes, but it all changes tonight—

at least for a little while. Come tomorrow morning, I'll wake up and everything will be back to normal. Back to missing him. Back to wishing I could be right there with him, wherever that might be. Back to waiting and anticipating.

It's too much. This past year has almost destroyed me, and there were times I wanted to give up. Times where I considered writing him one final letter and begging him to let me go. The truth is, this is absurd. What kind of woman waits around all year for a man she will see just once? I should be trying to move on. I should find someone to settle down with and do the whole big white house on a hill with a picket fence thing. I should think about my future. A wedding, kids, and a dog. Yet here I am in my lonely apartment, dressing up for a fictional man who holds my whole damn heart.

I truly am a sucker for punishment.

I've stayed up watching silly Christmas movies, each one of them ending with a happily ever after, and honestly, fuck them. Why do they get to have all their dreams come true when I only get to have one raunchy night per year? I mean, Nick doesn't even respond to my letters. Not that I have any idea how all of that shit is supposed to happen.

Has he even received my letters?

He told me to keep making Christmas wishes, and that's exactly what I did, but what if he's only getting the wish part of the letter? Nah, that's ridiculous. If he's getting the wish, then surely he's getting the letter. But fuck. Would it kill him to pick up a fucking pen and write me something in return? It's not as though I've been waiting on bated breath for him all damn year.

I get through a movie and a half before I finally turn it off and decide it's time to get ready. I have no idea what time to expect the dick-tator of my wettest dreams, but considering he still has to deliver a present to every single child in the whole damn universe, it could take a minute.

It's almost one in the morning, and as I adjust the bow around my waist and step into the black pumps that perfectly match my lingerie, a strange shiver trails down my spine, and though I can't explain it, I just know it's him.

The jitters hit me hard, and as I make my way out of my bedroom and into my living room, I quickly glance around, making sure that everything is perfect. I went hard on the Christmas decorations this year. I wanted everything to be perfect, and now my apartment looks like elves threw up in here. There's Christmas shit everywhere. Though by the time I'm through with him, it'll look a little more like a Santa sex-fest massacre. If cum isn't spread across the walls and the ceiling fan, then we did it wrong. But also, why the fuck am I so disgusting? Cum on my walls? What kind of sex-crazed monster has Nick turned me into?

Turning the light out, I keep the small lamp in my living room on, paired with the soft stream of moonlight shining through the window, and the mood lighting is just about perfect.

The nerves hit an all-time high, and I'm suddenly flooded with a wave of questions, every single one of them centered around how the hell I'm supposed to position myself.

Do I sit on the couch and try to look sexy with my legs apart, or is that too desperate? Do I take up residence on the coffee table? Do I hang out by my bedroom door and try to pose against the frame? What about the kitchen counter? Maybe I should just stand awkwardly in the middle of the room like I'm doing now.

Holy fucking shit.

Sheer panic rumbles through my chest. How did I manage to plan out every last second of tonight but forget about this? My gaze madly dances around my apartment, trying to figure myself out, when a shadow falls across my living room window, and suddenly nothing else matters.

The window pulls back and, within seconds, every glorious inch of my six-foot-four Christmas wish appears in my living room, his signature smirk staring back at me.

His eyes are so much darker than I remembered, and the butterflies deep in my stomach instantly soar. God, I've never been so happy in my life. He opens his arms, and every train of thought leaves me. All that matters is getting to him.

I run across my small apartment, my heels slamming against the hardwood floors, and I throw myself into the air, crashing into him with the force of a freight train.

His strong, capable arms lock around me as I twine my legs around his muscled waist. "Fuck, I've missed you," he rumbles as his lips crash down on mine.

I melt into him, and within seconds, he has my back against the living room wall, and intense pleasure rocks through my body. The butterflies turn to fire in my belly, and all I'm left with is a raw determination to feel him inside of me.

Hunger takes over as that familiar pine scent fills the air, intoxicating me with sheer need. My hands roam over his body, frantically pulling at his big red suit, and he hastily helps, holding onto me with only one hand as he reaches for the black belt around his waist.

"Oh God," I gasp as he holds me against the wall with his hips, grinding that thick cock against my core. "I need you inside me."

The belt falls to the floor, and the big red jacket is next to go, revealing his rock-hard body beneath. He's pure perfection. Every inch of his chest, arms, and abs are perfectly sculptured. I've never seen anything more delicious in my life.

"Nick, please," I groan.

He reaches down between us, freeing that delicious cock, and I can't help the way my tongue peeks out and rolls along my bottom lip, the raw desperation turning me into a frantic, caged animal. He wraps his fingers around the base of his cock, giving a firm squeeze as he pins me with his hips, freeing his other hand as I clutch onto him, trying to keep myself balanced against the wall.

Nick's other hand disappears between us, and the second his fingers brush over my needy cunt, a loud groan tears from the back of my throat. Who would have known that waiting twelve months to be touched by a man would do this to me? He quickly moves the fabric of my black thong aside and pushes his thick fingers inside me.

"Holy fuck," I moan, tipping my head back against the wall as I sense his wicked stare locked on my face. "Right there."

"You like that, baby?"

"God, yes."

"You're such a good girl, waiting all these months just for me."

Fuck. I love the way he talks to me, but I love that rich tone even more, and in response, all I can do is clench my walls around his fingers as he massages me from within.

"That's right, Mila. Squeeze my fingers. Show me how badly you need me."

"Fuck, Nick," I pant, my eyes coming back to his, and the moment our stares collide, fireworks burst between us, and the need is like nothing I've ever known. His lips crash back to mine, and he kisses me with an intensity that could set my whole damn apartment complex on fire.

He fucks me with his fingers, making sure I'm ready for him, but he should know better. I've been ready for him since Christmas Day last year. Every fucking day was absolute torture without him. The number of times I've had to fuck myself just to relieve the ache he left behind is absurd. I don't even want to begin to think about what my neighbors must think of me.

His thumb stretches up to my clit, and just that slight pressure is enough to set me off, my hips wildly jolting against his hold, and as Nick demands full control of my body, I come apart, my orgasm coming out of nowhere and rocking my whole damn world. I come on his fingers, my walls erratically spasming around him, but he doesn't let up or stop rolling his fingers against my walls, curving and splitting them as I throw my head back with sheer satisfaction.

It's too much, and my eyes start to roll. "That's right, Mila. Come for me. Let me feel how you squeeze me."

His words are intoxicating, and I know without a doubt that this man will be the death of me. But death by intense orgasm seems like the ultimate way to go.

"Holy fucking shit," I groan, my nails digging into his strong shoulder, leaving little half-moons in his flawless skin.

Nick's fingers continue their pleasure-filled assault on my pussy, and as my orgasm flows through my veins and sends my world into a blissful abyss, I feel his lips come down on the sensitive skin of my neck.

It's the best moment of my life, and I swear, for just a moment, I feel the whole fucking world shake beneath us. "Oh, God. Nick," I groan as my fingers twine into his hair, holding on to him for dear life. Then as the intensity of my orgasm begins to fizzle out, he pulls his fingers free and takes my hips, holding me tight against the wall.

"You ready for me, Mila?" he questions, holding my hungry stare, but he already knows the answer to that. He can feel how fucking ready I am.

"I've never been so ready," I tell him through heaving breaths. Then in a blinding thrust, Nick slams his thick cock inside of me, and as my walls stretch around his sheer size, we both fucking crumble.

"Fuck," he grunts, his fingers tighten on my hips as he takes a second to find himself. "You've got no fucking idea how much I've needed this."

I can't help but laugh. "Probably about as much as I have," I say, only my voice comes out as a strained whisper. "I need you to move, Nick. Please. Don't keep me waiting."

He doesn't hesitate, and as his hips rock, my eyelids flutter, the pleasure already too much for me to handle. But I trust Nick, and despite how intense this is going to be, he'll be right there holding me up.

His hips slam forward again, and I cry out, almost positive the sheer intensity of his frantic thrusts will shake the whole fucking building, but that's exactly what I asked for, isn't it? I need my world rocked in a way I'll never recover from.

Nick starts to truly fuck me, pinning me against the wall as his hips pull back and roll forward, taking me at every angle. It's exhilarating. I've never felt anything so animalistic and raw, and I fucking love it. I love his wild need for me, and I love how it matches my wild need for him.

"Damn it, Mila. You're so fucking perfect for me."

I can't respond as he blows my mind. I'm able to feel everything, right down to the bulbous head of his cock and the angry veins as he slams in and out of me.

"You have no fucking idea how many times I've had to fuck myself, picturing the way you would ride me tonight. How you'd take me in your mouth and make me come until I came down your pretty little throat. Just the words in your letters had me falling to pieces. I've never been so desperate in my life."

Hmmm. Just the thought of watching him making himself come does wicked things to me.

"Fuck. Is it too late to wish I could see the way you fuck yourself?"

A wicked grin stretches across his face, and the way his eyes shimmer with happiness is enough to keep me fulfilled for the next twelve months without him. "I think I can make time for that."

A laugh bubbles up my throat, but before the sound can fly out of me, I grab Nick and pull him back in until his lips are firmly against mine. He kisses me deeply, his tongue swiping through my mouth as his hand slides up my waist, not stopping until he's reached the curve of my breast.

He pulls the cup down just enough for my nipple to peek out the top and the way he takes it between his skilled fingers and gently rolls it sends pulsing shots of electricity right down to my core.

I crumble in his strong arms, my whole body falling to pieces around him as everything that I am becomes his. I wasn't sure during the year if I was actually falling for this man or if it was all in my head, but having him here in the flesh, I know for sure. I am unequivocally in love with him.

He takes me deep, and I cling to him with a need that makes my heart race faster than it ever has. "Nick," I pant.

"I know," he tells me, his voice so soft, so sure. Then as it becomes all too much, I detonate again, only this time, Nick is right there with me, shooting hot spurts of cum deep inside me.

His fingers tighten on my body as he comes, and I hold him closer, crying out in absolute ecstasy. My orgasm pulses through me, claiming every single inch of my body, right through to my fingers and toes, and I can't help but throw my head back against the wall as I shatter like glass.

Nick doesn't stop, his thick cock moving in and out of me in long, determined thrusts, and I know without a doubt that he feels the way my pussy convulses around him.

God, I've needed this so much.

A deep groan rumbles through his chest, and the sound of his pleasure is enough to set me alight all over again. "Holy shit," I pant, as he drops his forehead to my shoulder, taking deep breaths as we both start coming down from our high.

"You can say that again," he says, and as a proud smirk stretches across my lips, I make a point to squeeze my walls and laugh at the way he groans again. "Fuck, baby. You're going to be the reason I fall to my knees."

"You have no idea how okay I am with that."

Nick laughs and shifts his hands to my ass before pulling me away from the wall. The slight movement causes him to shift inside me, making my sensitive body jolt. He walks us over to my kitchen and places my ass down on the counter before gently pulling himself free.

He takes the slightest step back before bracing his hands against the counter and caging me in, his dark stare locked so firmly on mine. "I'm fucking serious, Mila. You've got no idea how desperately I've craved everything you are this year. Walking away from you last December fucking destroyed me. I don't know how I'm supposed to do it again."

"Then don't."

"It's not that easy, Mila. I'm in love with you. Have been since I was eight years old," he tells me, making my heart run a million miles an hour as his hand shifts to my bare thigh. "I know you wanted clarity about you and me and how all of this is supposed to work, but I really don't know how I'm supposed to give you that. All I can tell you is that I've been yours since before I can fucking remember."

I nod, my fingers dancing across his chest and down to his hand on my thigh. "I love you, too."

He holds my stare a moment longer before dipping his head toward mine and kissing me again, and this time, it's different from earlier. It's not the hungry need of two people desperate to come alive. It's almost a heartbroken kind of kiss, both of us knowing that this thing between us can never go anywhere further than this, despite how we feel for each other.

Not wanting to kill the mood of our one night together, I slowly pull back and place my hand against his warm chest. "I believe you have a list of wishes that require marking off."

A stupid grin pulls at the corner of his lips, and he wastes no time pulling the printout of wishes from his pocket before handing it to me. I quickly scan over it, realizing he's already ticked a few boxes. "Wow, you're certainly not wasting any time," I tease before glancing around my kitchen in search of a pen. "Looks like January, March, and November are already out of the way."

"Then what are you waiting for?" he says, reaching for a pen that I clearly missed. "Tick them off."

A wide smile settles on my face as I get to work, ticking off the first three boxes of the night.

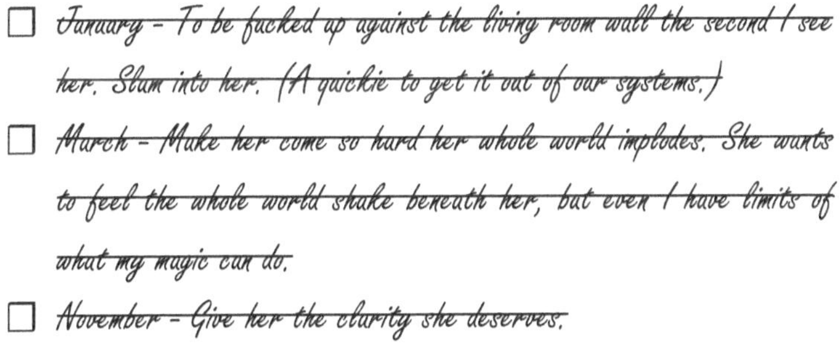

"You know, there's an awful lot of things to get through," I comment, glancing over the list one more time, hardly able to even remember making some of these wishes, but I won't lie, I like the sound of every last one of them. "Do you think we'll have time to get through them all?"

Nick arches a brow. "Do you doubt me, Mila?"

All I can do is shake my head as he takes the list from my hand and places it down on the counter beside me. "Time is of the essence. We better get to work."

A thrill shoots through me as his dark, hungry gaze sails over my body, taking in my lingerie and the big red bow around my waist. "Did I tell you how fucking gorgeous you are? Just the sight of you like this . . . How did I ever get so lucky?"

My cheeks flush, but as his gaze comes back to mine, something shifts in his dark stare. "It's a shame I'm going to have to unwrap you."

"Oh?" I ask, the butterflies soaring deep in my stomach. "And just how do you intend to do that?"

He pinches the bow around my waist between his fingers, and I watch as it slowly begins to unravel, and with every passing second, his gaze darkens even more. It's the most erotic thing I've ever seen, but when he lays me back against the counter and takes the sheer material of my thong between his teeth and begins dragging it down my thighs, the thrill that rushes through me is simply delicious.

He pulls my thong right off over my black heels, and I make a mental note to tick off December's wish of watching him remove my underwear with his teeth. But holy fuck, I also need to make a mental note to add that as a standing wish for every single Christmas to come because that was hot.

I sit back up on the counter as Nick drops to his knees, and as my stomach begins to do flip-flops, Nick slowly spreads my thighs. He scoops his arms beneath my thighs, pulling me right to the edge of the counter and I quickly catch myself on my palms before I fall back.

"Mmmm," Nick groans, inhaling deeply. "You smell divine."

My cheeks flush again. I can't say I've ever had a man smell me, but when it comes to Nick, I just take it as it comes.

I can't help but watch as his fingers trail through my wetness, teasing my opening and mixing with his cum. Then just when it becomes too much, he slowly pushes himself back inside of me before curving his fingers and rolling them over my g-spot time and time again.

My body shudders, and when he looks up at me with that cocky smirk and dark, shimmering eyes, he knows he's got me right where he wants me. "You like that, Mila?" he murmurs. "Do you like how I fuck you with my fingers?"

I nod, biting my bottom lip, the anticipation boiling inside me, knowing exactly what comes next.

"Tell me what you want."

"Don't stop."

He shakes his head. "Come on, baby. Tell me what you really want. Don't be shy. We both know what a whore you are for me. Don't hold back now."

I'm sure my cheeks are blazing by this point, but he has a point. This is the only man on earth who knows just how desperately I want to be fucked, yet he's also the only one who can do it in a way that will make my whole world implode. I can't hold back from him.

My fingers brush across my skin, trailing over my exposed nipple and down between my thighs before slowly circling my needy clit. "I want you to fuck me with your mouth, Nick. Flick my clit with your tongue and make me come on your fingers again. Treat me like your filthy whore. Make me come for you."

He dives into me, his warm mouth closing over my clit, not leaving me a single second to remove my hand, and as my fingers roll over my clit, so does his tongue. "Oh God," I groan, unable to tear my stare away. His tongue rolls out of his mouth and circles my clit, all while his fingers rotate inside of me, massaging my walls.

I pull my fingers away, letting him get to work, and fuck, does he ever!

Nick is too much, too good, and I don't know how to handle it, but I better figure it out soon because this is only the beginning of our night. We still have a million more months to tick off.

He goes hard, eating my pussy as though he hasn't eaten all year, and there's no doubt about it, he takes pride in his work. You can always tell when a man eats pussy because he has to, compared to when a man eats pussy because he thoroughly enjoys it, and jolly old Saint Nicholas here is the latter. All he wants is to see me come, and getting to be the one who makes me shatter is the only gift on his wish list. But he should know by now that I give as good as I get, and judging by tonight's performance, he's in for one hell of a ride tonight.

He takes his time, pushing me right to the edge before pulling back and drawing out my orgasm, each time getting even more intense.

My walls contract around his fingers, desperate to come as my ability to cry out and groan leaves me. I'm speechless and completely at his mercy, just waiting for him to let me come, but he doesn't. He's intent on drawing out every second of my pleasure, claiming it for himself, even if it takes all night.

I'm so fucking close. So desperate, but he increases the intensity each time, working me and working me until I can't hold in my cries a second longer. "FUCK!" I scream out, throwing my head back as my hands ball into tight fists on the counter. "Fuck. Nick, please. I need to come."

His tongue rolls over my clit once more, sucking and nipping as he picks up the pace of his fingers, and I feel his wicked smile against my pussy. "You need to come, baby?" he murmurs against me.

"You know I do," I pant.

He laughs to himself before finally giving me what I've been needing, circling my clit with his tongue as his fingers plunge deeper. Only this time, he doesn't just push me toward the edge, he grabs me and launches me right off it.

"OH FUCK!" I cry out, clutching the back of his head and holding him right there between my thighs as his tongue does its filthy magic and sends me into a whole other universe. I see stars dancing across my vision as every nerve ending inside my body buzzes with electricity.

My toes curl inside my heels, and as Nick keeps working my body, I'm left solely to his mercy.

CHAPTER 10

MILA

Is it possible for your body to physically melt after such an intense orgasm? Because I'm almost positive that's exactly what's happening to me right now.

"Holy fucking shit, Nick," I breathe, barely able to catch my breath as he straightens to his full height, and even with me sitting up on the kitchen counter, he still towers over me.

He's such a man. So beautifully sculptured. It's impossible not to be so immensely attracted to him. Just the sight of his body is enough to send me into a tailspin.

He places his hands on either side of my thighs, just like he did when he first put me here, only this time, I'm the one falling apart, and I drop my head against his chest, barely able to keep myself upright.

"Are you okay?" he murmurs, lifting a hand to my back and slowly trailing it up and down.

"Yeah, I just need a minute," I tell him. "That was more than I expected. I mean, shit, Nick. Is it possible to die by orgasm? I've never felt anything so . . . intense before. I thought I was actually going to crumble."

"My bad," he says with a proud smirk. "I had to outdo last year's performance."

I roll my eyes. "Last year's performance was already incredible. I didn't think it was possible to outdo it, but I suppose it's part of your job description to make the impossible happen."

Nick winks. "Jolly old Saint Nick at your service, ma'am."

I can't help but laugh. "I thought you said Saint Nicholas is what your dad prefers to go by."

"Yeah, I did," he says with an awkward cringe, the laughter quickly fading out of his tone. "It felt wrong the second it came out of my mouth."

I shake my head, falling more and more in love with this man by the second, and fuck, I'm glad it's him. With every word out of his mouth, I get to know the real him better, and I absolutely adore the man I'm getting to know.

"Come on," he says a moment later, scooping his strong arms beneath my thighs and lifting me off the counter. He starts to make his way to the living room when I suck in a gasp and look back toward the kitchen.

"Wait. The list. I have to mark some things off."

Nick chuckles to himself and performs a U-turn back to the kitchen. I almost tumble right out of his arms as I dive for the pen and paper, and the moment I'm securely back in his embrace, I glance down the list again.

"I think it's safe to say that both February and December are deserving of being marked off," I say as he lowers us onto my couch, and I immediately shift around to get comfortable before ending up straddled over his lap.

I get to work ticking off boxes.

☐ *February – Head over to the kitchen counter and give the walls something to talk about! (More specifically, fuck her with my tongue.) Spread her creamy thighs and go to town with my mouth. Show her how fucking great it can be.*

☐ *December – Lay her down and tear her lingerie off with my teeth.*

"Oh, and just so you know," I say, glancing up with burning cheeks. "Tearing my underwear off with your teeth is going on next year's wish list too. And the year after that. Actually, let's put it down for the next ten years and then we'll revisit it."

Nick's touch is feather light as he palms my waist, and it's hard to believe that his strong, capable hands can be this gentle. It's as though I'm the most precious gemstone in the world, and he's terrified of breaking me.

"Next ten years, huh?"

"And more," I say, all too confidently. "Assuming you don't get bored of me and go find some other girl to spend your Christmas Eves with."

Nick scoffs. "I don't think you understand that when I say I've loved you since I was eight years old, just how infatuated I've been. No other woman has ever held my attention. It's only ever been you. I spend every year waiting to see you again, and then when I'm finally with you, I spend the whole time dreading saying goodbye. There will never be any other girl for me. Even if you decide to eventually move on and start a family with some other guy, I'll still be here, hoping like hell that you'll still let me see you every Christmas, even if it's just to sit in your room and watch you sleep like I used to."

My heart swells in my chest as an incredible warmth spreads through me. "I don't think I could ever be with anyone else after this. Even during those long, lonely months, I couldn't take my mind off you. I just don't understand it. How can I feel so strongly about a man I've only met once?"

"When your soul finds its person, it knows," he tells me. "You're my person, Mila. There's no point even trying with someone else when I've known it's been you since I was a kid."

"Why didn't you ever wake me up? For twenty years you just sat in my room and watched me sleep. Why didn't you ever introduce yourself? We could have had years together."

He shakes his head. "I couldn't. I wasn't going to wake you up and demand that you love me. I needed you to come to me. I needed you to feel it first, and the moment you did, I wasn't holding back."

Taking his shoulder, I push up onto my knees before leaning in and kissing him once again. "Thank you," I murmur against his full lips, appreciating him giving me the time I needed over the years. "I don't know what this is or how we're supposed to navigate it, but it's more than I could ever ask for. I just . . . I have one question."

"What's that?"

"Is this all in my head? Are you only here ticking off all these wishes because I wished for it? I mean, what if I never wished for you to touch me?"

A smile pulls at the corners of his lips, and the way his eyes light up has my heart in overspeed. "Trust me, Mila. I've never really been one to follow the rules. I would have figured out a way to have you. This is as real as it gets, and I'm not about to let you go."

My eyes fill with tears of happiness, and I quickly blink them away, embarrassed about just how emotional I'm getting with all of this. Though it's not like he can blame me. It's the best night of my life, after all. And with that, I discreetly grab the wish list and tick off April's wish, more than satisfied with how he's made my heart come alive.

☑ *April – Make her feel something. Can be creative with this. And no, she doesn't mean with my cock. She wants her heart to come alive.*

Putting the list down beside me, I decide to take this into my own hands. "So, May's wish?"

He arches a brow. "The bright red mold of my dick?" I grin, and he continues. "Now, why would such an innocent thing like yourself need one of those?"

"Don't tell me you didn't do it."

Nick laughs and takes my waist, lifting me off him before getting to his feet and making his way over to the living room window where a massive, bright red dildo rests on the window frame. I don't know how the hell I missed it, but fuck, there it is, and it's absolutely beautiful.

"You don't want to know the kind of hell I went through to get this," he tells me, taking it off the window frame and making his way back to me. "Making a mold of your cock is a shitload harder than it ought to be, especially when you have your mother knocking on the door and wondering why you're not answering."

A laugh bursts from my chest. "Tell me you're lying?"

"I really wish I could, but don't worry. The thought of watching you use it got me through it."

"Oh yeah?" I ask, trying not to imagine the way he would have had to stick his cock into a tube filled with molding clay. "And just how often have you pictured me using it?"

"Only every single moment of every single day since you first mentioned it in May."

He sits down on the couch beside me, and my self-control flies out the window as I snatch the bright red dildo out of his hands. "Wow," I say, looking over it as closely as possible. "It's exactly the same, and you even got the veins in there."

"I wouldn't want to disappoint you, now would I?"

"Oh no. Believe me, disappointing me would usually result in you being edged in the same way you just did to me, only you wouldn't get the happy ending like I did."

"Damn. That's brutal."

"Uh-huh," I agree. "But you have been more than pleasing so far, so I assume maybe you might get what you've been wanting after all."

His brow arches again. "Oh yeah?"

My tongue rolls over my bottom lip as excitement drums through me, and I hastily get to my feet before taking the two quick steps to my coffee table and slamming the red dildo down right in the center. I'll have to remember to thank him for remembering to make it with a suction cup on the bottom. That's going to be extremely useful.

Nick watches me with a blazing stare. "And what exactly do you plan on doing with that?"

A stupid grin stretches across my face as I slowly begin to circle the coffee table. "Why don't you let me worry about that? You just sit back and relax, maybe you'll get a chance to show me how you work yourself after all."

And with that, I climb onto the coffee table before positioning myself over the red mold of Nick's dick and slowly begin to sink down onto it. He slowly sucks in a breath as the cool silicone begins to stretch me, and I sink the whole way down, groaning with how full I am.

"Holy fuck," I murmur under my breath before slowly rising up on my knees again and loving the way Nick has become completely mesmerized by the way I ride the replica of him. My fingers join the party, rolling over my clit, and when Nick leans back on my couch and slips his hand inside his pants, fisting his massive cock, I almost come apart.

I put on a show, letting him see just how well I ride his replica, giving him the best possible view. The way he can't tear his eyes off me is too much. He makes me come alive and makes my skin dance with goosebumps.

"Fuck, baby. You're so damn gorgeous when you ride me like that."

All I can do is smile as I tilt my head back, letting him see even more of me. "Show me how you work yourself," I breathe, my eyes locked on him just as surely as his are locked on me.

Nick doesn't hesitate to free his cock from the confines of his pants, and he shows me exactly how he likes to stroke himself. Slowly moving up and down his impressive length before circling his tip. He's rock-hard, and the more I bounce up and down on his replica, the angrier his cock seems to get.

He groans, so close to the edge, but he clearly needs more. My tongue swipes across my bottom lip. "Come here," I tell him, and within seconds, he's on his feet, moving toward me.

His cock stares me right in the face, and hunger fills me as Nick brushes my hair back over my shoulder, bunching it into his fist. With my free hand, I wrap my fingers around the base of his cock, guiding it into my mouth.

I open wide, taking him right down the back of my throat as I continue riding his replica cock. It's too much, but I absolutely love it.

"Mmmm, just like that, baby," he groans, his tone so fucking deep that my pussy clenches around the red dildo. "Show me how deep you can take me."

I push him further into the back of my throat, and each time I come back, I tease him with my tongue, rolling it over his tip as I suck hard. With one hand, I pump up and down his massive length, and with the other, my fingers circle my clit.

Nick tightens his hold in my hair, and I move a little faster, bouncing up and down on the dildo as I suck him harder. Tears spring to my eyes as I push past my gag-reflex, but I ignore it, desperate to show him just how far I'm willing to go for him. Whatever he's willing to give, I'm willing to take.

"Fuck, Mila," he growls through a clenched jaw.

I grin against his cock as a pleasure-filled moan rips through my chest. I'm so close to the edge. My fingers keep working, rolling tight circles over my clit, and I sink down even lower on Nick's replica, taking it so deep, I can almost feel him in my stomach.

My walls begin to shake, and I clench my pussy, the desperation just about ready to claim me, but I don't dare stop, pushing myself to my limits. Nick pulls himself free from my mouth and comes, shooting his hot load all over my throat and tits.

Heat booms through me. I didn't expect that, but I loved it, and with his cum all over me, I finally let myself relax, my orgasm exploding from within me. "Oh shit," I groan, grinding down on the cock as my walls begin to spasm.

I bring myself to a stop, trying to catch my breath, but Nick simply shakes his head. "Oh, baby. It's sweet you think you're done," he says, whipping me around on the coffee table and bending me over, the replica cock still buried deep inside of me.

"I'm going to take your sweet ass, Mila. Just like you asked."

I suck in a gasp. I was hoping for this, but I didn't really know how to approach it.

"Tell me, baby. Did you prepare yourself for this just like you said you would?"

I swallow over the lump in my throat and nod as I glance back over my shoulder. With my cum-covered tits flat against the coffee table, I lift my ass high in the air for the taking as his replica cock still stretches my pussy wide.

He simply stares at me, shaking his head as if in disbelief about what he sees, and I can only imagine what I look like to him right now. "Take me, Nick. I'm all yours, just be gentle with me."

"Always," he grumbles, fisting his cock with one hand before using his other to tease me. His fingers dance through my wetness, mixing with the mess of cum leaking between me and the replica cock, and with every swipe of his fingers, my body jolts.

I'm so fucking sensitive right now, but I love it. Anything could set me off, and when Nick presses his wet fingers to my ass, I realize this is going to be a quick one.

He quickly gets me ready, teasing my ass as I push back against his fingers, desperate to take more. I don't stop watching him, my eyes glued to the way he slowly strokes himself, not letting himself get too carried away. But let's be honest, we're both already on the edge.

I grind down against the silicon cock, every slight movement driving me wild, and when he finally pushes his fingers inside and begins to stretch me, my eyes roll. "Oh shit, Nick."

"That okay?"

"I need more. I need you."

"Are you sure?"

"Yes. Please."

"Mmmm, that's my good girl," he says, adjusting himself right behind me before lifting my hips and forcing the silicone cock to fall out of me. He slides into my pussy, his cock mixing with the mess of cum, and when he pulls out, he lets me lower back down onto the silicone cock.

I feel his tip right at my ass, and a thrill of excitement booms through me. I've never been so forward with what I want, but why the hell not? I thought we might go down this path tonight, but never in a million years did I think we'd do it with me already riding his replica. I'm already so stretched, but something tells me I haven't seen anything yet.

He begins to push inside of me, and I suck in a gasp, feeling as I begin to stretch, and I do my best to relax around his size. Don't get me wrong, I purposefully got the biggest dildo I could find to practice and prepare myself for tonight, but it's got nothing on him.

I'm ready though.

He takes me inch by inch, taking his time. "Rub your clit, Mila. It'll help you relax around me."

I do as he asks, slipping my hand between my legs and gently rolling my fingers over my clit. Pulling in a few deep, calming breaths, I let myself relax around him until the burn begins to feel almost welcoming.

Holy shit.

This is good.

"Okay," I finally say, getting a little too confident and slowly moving up and down the dildo at the same time. "I can take more."

"I know you can."

He pushes deeper into me until I feel him finally bottoming out, and when he sucks in a breath, I know I've got him right where I want him. "Fuck me, Nick," I beg him. "Claim all of me. Let me be a whore for you."

His fingers dig into my hips, and I welcome the burn. When he shifts his hips, my eyes roll to the back of my head. "Holy fucking shit."

"You've got that right," he mutters through a clenched jaw.

My fingers keep rolling over my clit to help my muscles stay relaxed, and when he really starts to move, I realize what I've been missing out on all these years. I've never felt so full in my life. His movements are enough to rock me back and forth, my body making short pulses over the dildo. Every nerve ending comes alive. I've never experienced so much pleasure all at once, and I don't know what to do with it.

He moves back and forth, being gentle while also taking me deep. It sets my body on fire in the best way. "Oh God, Nick. Yes," I groan, my free hand clutching the side of the coffee table so tight that my knuckles turn white. "Don't stop."

He reaches over me and twists my hair into his hand again, pulling back against my hair and forcing me to arch my back. My cum-covered tits lift off the coffee table, and I cry out with the sweetest pleasure. The angle I take both him and the dildo shifts, and I'm launched into a whole new world of ecstasy.

"Shit. Nick, I . . . I can't. I'm going to come."

"Give it to me, Mila. Squeeze me. Show me how you come for me."

"Fuck."

He slams into me one more time, and my hips jolt, grinding me down over the dildo and massaging my walls from within, and as my fingers roll over my needy clit, I can't hold onto it a second longer. My world detonates, and I crumble into a million tiny pieces as my orgasm rocks through me, taking me on the sweetest high.

"Oh fuck, yes," I cry out.

Nick comes with me, both of us shattering as we come for the millionth time tonight. Hell, I've lost count of the number of times he's enticed a soul-shattering orgasm out of me and made the world shake beneath my feet.

Taking pity on my poor body, Nick doesn't drag this one out, instead, he comes to a stop, giving me instant relief as we both crumble. He slowly pulls back, and the moment he's free I let out a breath as my body fully relaxes, despite the red replica being as deep as humanly possible.

My face rests against the coffee table, and at this point, I'm too exhausted to even care about the cum now squished between me and the table. It'll start getting overly sticky soon, and when that happens, I can guarantee that I'm not going to want to be here. I just don't have enough energy to care right now.

"You okay?" Nick asks, his fingers trailing along my spine.

"Uh-huh," is all I can manage to say.

"Come on," he laughs. "Let me shower you and then we'll see about ticking a few more things off your wish list." And with that, he scoops me up, leaving the dildo suction cupped to the coffee table, gently swaying back and forth.

CHAPTER 11

MILA

After wrapping my silk gown around me, I scramble into my bed beside Nick, the exhaustion of the night quickly claiming me, but as long as he's here, I'll fight it. I won't waste a single second of the night by accidentally falling asleep.

I nuzzle into Nick's side, desperately wishing that things could be like this all the time, and while we've ticked plenty of things off our list, I can't help but feel as though our time together is quickly coming to an end.

"What do we have left?" he questions, though something tells me he knows exactly what's on this list. He doesn't need the reminder, he's just trying to keep my mind from going somewhere it shouldn't.

"Let's see, shall we?"

Reaching over Nick, I get the list and pen off my bedside table and try to work out how it got there when I was positive I left them on the couch, but at some point, I have to remember that when I'm with Nick, the impossible tends to happen.

Glancing over the list, I tick off the few things we just accomplished on my coffee table.

- [ ] *May – A perfect mold of my veiny dick, preferably in bright Christmas red. Don't forget the veins! Batteries not included.*
- [ ] *August – Bend her over and take her from behind, hand in her hair, and don't dare hold back. Be rough with her. Then let her ride the replica cock while I fuck her mouth.*
- [ ] *September – Claim that sweet ass if she's up for it. Take it slow. She's new at this.*
- [ ] *October – Surprise her. Give her something she's not expecting. One pearl necklace coming right up.*

"You really didn't hold back with that pearl necklace, huh?"

"No, I can't say that I did, but you asked for a surprise, and I figured what better surprise than a pearl necklace?"

"Good point," I say, before pausing, my hand hovering over the list. "Wait. I ticked August's wish for bending me over and doing me from behind, but like . . . what just happened on the coffee table still counts, right? Even though I was intending on that being a pussy taking and not an ass claiming?"

"Uhhhh, I think it still counts," he says, glancing over the list again. "I mean, I still bent you over and took you from behind, and there was nothing in the wish that specified which hole that was intended for."

"Ahh, perfect."

Don't get me wrong, if it didn't count, I'm more than happy to do it again until we can mark it off properly, but I simply don't have enough energy right now. Especially considering there's still one more ride for me to take.

"So, in July when you wished to get to know me better, what kind of things were you wanting to know?"

"Oh, ummm . . . wow. Talk about pressure, huh? I feel like there's so much I want to know about you, but not enough time to cover everything."

"What do you feel is most important to you?"

"I want to know your heart," I tell him. "What kind of man are you? What was your childhood like? Do the people back home actually like you or do they tolerate you just because you're the big man in red? What are your parents like? Oh, and how do you know how to fuck so well? Have you been doing all the little elves because that's kinda weird, right?"

"Woah," he laughs. "Slow down."

I can't help but laugh too, and I find myself sitting up beside him, just like I did last year, eager to know everything about him.

"I don't really know where to start with all of that, but I suppose as for the kind of man I am. I guess only you can answer that. You're the only one I've ever allowed to get close enough."

My brows furrow, surprised by that considering how little I already know of him, which speaks volumes about the relationships he has with other people. "What about your parents?"

"They see me as the fuck-up child I always was, and to be honest, I was only that way because I was angry with the world. I wanted to be here with you. Being isolated sent me down a dark spiral. I was an asshole for a long time and a real dick to those who didn't deserve it. So yeah, I suppose that answers your other question. Most people just tolerate me because they're scared I'm going to be an asshole, which is fair, but over these past twelve months, I'd dare say things have gotten better."

"So your parents only tolerate you."

"No. Mom and Dad have always been great. Mom sees the best in people and is pretty much exactly who all those bullshit Christmas movies make her out to be. She's a sweet old lady who just wants to bake shortbread."

"And your dad?"

"He's a little more complicated. He sees me as the black sheep of the family and has trouble trusting me not to fuck things up. But I've more than proven to him that I can still do my job and have you too."

"Oh, so he knows you've been coming here?"

Nick nods. "He doesn't just know that I'm here, he's read through your list of wishes."

My eyes bulge out of my head. I know he mentioned that his father saw my wish last year, but that doesn't seem as horrifying as the detailed wishes I made this year. "Oh my god," I say, squishing my hands over my face as my cheeks begin to burn with embarrassment. "He must think I'm a skank trying to corrupt his son."

"No," Nick laughs. "If anything, he thinks I'm the big asshole who's corrupted this sweet little girl he used to gift dolls to."

"Holy shit."

I collapse into the sheets beside him, burying my face into the pillows as he laughs. "It's fine, he really doesn't care that much. He knows we have an . . . odd relationship, and he's okay with it. As long as I don't fall behind in my duties, then we're all good."

"Okay," I murmur, getting comfortable against his chest. "And as for all those little whore elves you've been screwing."

Nick laughs. "Am I going to break your heart if I tell you there are no elves in the North Pole? That's just some ridiculous myth the media made up, and the rest of the world ran with it. The workshop has thousands of helpers, who are human, by the way. And yes, on occasion, I've found myself having a little fun with a few of them. But not since having you."

"Just been you and your hand then?"

"Your letters certainly helped with some visualization."

A laugh bubbles up my throat, and I place my hand on his chest, feeling the thrum of his heart beneath. "I don't want you to go," I tell him, fearing what comes next.

"I know," he says, reaching over to me and lifting me until I'm straddled over him. "It's only a year before I see you again."

"A year is a very long time."

He nods, and I know he feels it just as much as I do.

"I wish things could always be like this."

Tears form in my eyes, and he pulls me in closer, closing the gap between us as his lips come down on mine. He kisses me deeply, and just like before, I can't help but feel as though it's some kind of fucked-up goodbye. "If there were a way," he says against my lips, letting his sentence fall flat.

"I know," I whisper.

A single tear rolls down my cheek, and Nick quickly captures it before wiping it away. "We have now, Mila," he tells me, seeming conflicted about something, but aren't we both?

He's right though. We have now, and I don't want to waste it crying over missing him when he hasn't even left yet. I should be making the most of it, and that's exactly what I do when I crush my lips back to his. I kiss him deeper, this time being the one to take control as my tongue sweeps into his mouth.

He hardens beneath me, and I grind down against him, feeling myself getting wetter by the second. Only something tells me this one is going to be different. It's not going to be the wild, animalistic fucking from out in the living room and against the wall. This one is just him and me with our hearts both on the line.

His lips move to my neck and I close my eyes, feeling the raw pleasure pulsing through my veins. "I'm not ready to miss you," I tell him, feeling my eyes begin to fill with tears all over again.

"Then don't miss me, Mila. Be happy knowing I will come back. Don't grieve me leaving, anticipate my next arrival."

His words make it sound so simple, but we both know it's really not. He's been right where I am. He knows how it feels to say goodbye knowing that you won't see the other for another twelve months. And yet, all I can do is smile against his lips as he kisses me. "You're so full of shit."

Nick laughs, and I rise up onto my knees. His arm locks around my back, holding me to him, and as he takes his cock in his other hand, I slowly sink down onto him. I groan, feeling a slight ache from the already crazy night of sex, but I'm not about to give in now.

My list specifies that I need to ride him until he comes, and I'm not about to give up on that one. After all, making him come deep inside of me is my favorite thing to do.

I rock my hips and grind against him as our lips fuse together, each of us soaking in the moment, not willing to let this go just yet. Our bodies move in unison, both of us panting as he grips my hips, but he knows the rules for this one. He's not allowed to take control. He can only lay back and take it until he falls apart.

I take him the way I like, clenching my walls around him and letting him feel just how desperately I want him as I rise and fall over his cock. Then grabbing the headboard, I lean into him, and when he captures my nipple in his mouth over my silk gown, I should have known better. Nick admitted that he's a natural rule breaker. I should have seen this coming. Hell, I should be grateful he's allowed me to maintain control, but I don't doubt that soon enough, he's going to take that control for himself.

Nick flicks his tongue over my nipple, and I feel the hot pulses right down to my core. I can't help but arch into him, silently asking for more. He gives in, giving me exactly what I've asked for, and as he does it again, I let out a desperate moan. "Fuck, Nick. You're everything I need."

I bounce over his cock, clenching with each rise and fall, and as his hand drops between us and torments my clit with his sweet fingers, I feel that familiar tightening deep inside of me. "Oh God."

Nick's hands tighten on my body, and as I circle my hips, his kisses become more frantic. "Fuck, Mila. I have to take you."

I grin against his lips, loving the way my pussy is tormenting him. "Ask nicely."

"Mila," he growls, on the fucking edge.

I grin again, and this time he knows it's my way of giving in, and within the blink of an eye, I'm on my back with Nick's arm scooped beneath my knee, hitching it up as high as it'll go. He rolls his hips back and in a flash, he's thrusting deep inside of me, taking me at a whole new angle. "Oh God," I groan, sucking in a deep gasp.

He closes his eyes, and I watch as his jaw tightens. "Fuck, Mila. I will never get enough of being inside of you."

"More," I beg.

He pulls back and thrusts again, and this time we both lose our minds. My legs start to shake, and I wrap my arms around his strong back, digging my nails into his beautiful skin. His lips come down on my neck as his other hand slips inside my gown and cups my breast, his thumb and forefinger gently rolling over my nipple.

The pleasure is too much, and as it all comes together, I come one final time, my orgasm pulsing through me like molten lava, claiming every single inch of me. Nick comes with me, shooting his hot load deep inside me, and as we both come down from our high, the heaviness comes along with it, and all I can do is hold him against me.

He rolls us so that I lay over his chest, his big arms wrapped so securely around me that I never want to let go. We lay in silence, both of us lost in thought, and when I reach for the crumpled list on the sheets, I let out a heavy sigh.

Pushing up onto Nick's chest, I lay the list on his chest and try to flatten out the crumpled paper. Don't get me wrong, I'm so glad we were able to do all the wild and exciting things on this list, but a part of me wishes it was so much longer so that he never had to leave. I could keep him chained up here for the rest of time as a sex slave. I mean, sure, it might be frowned upon to keep a sex slave chained to your bed, maybe slightly illegal, but I'm sure if I ran the idea past Nick, he'd be down for it. As long as I offer the occasional meal to keep those energy levels up, then we should be good.

Finding the pen somewhere under the pillow, I mark off the two final proper wishes before letting my gaze sail over the very last one.

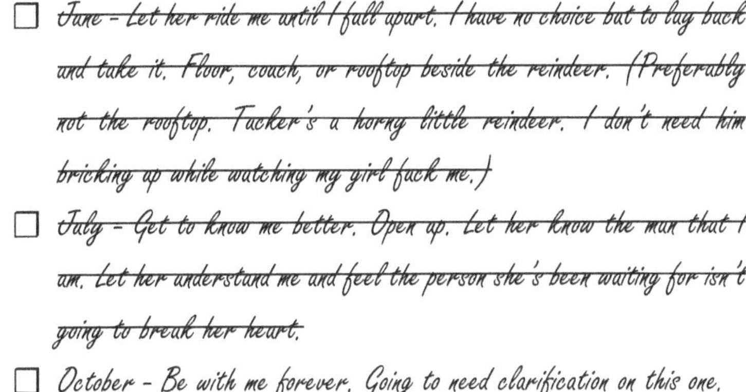

Be with me forever. It's not a realistic wish, and I think we both know that. To be honest, I barely remember making the wish. It's just one of those things that roll off the tongue. And in this case, rolled off the pen. I was simply writing the thoughts running rampant in my mind, but it doesn't make it any less true. But how could it ever be? He's Santa Claus for fuck's sake.

His world is . . . I don't even know where his world is. Is the North Pole supposed to be somewhere near Antarctica? No, wait. That's the southern hemisphere. Surely the North Pole is somewhere, well . . . north. Right?

"What's going through your mind, Mila?"

"Where is the North Pole?" I ask. "Can I maybe . . . I don't know, visit? Is that weird?"

Nick laughs, his hand lowering down my back until his large

palm is resting against my ass. "It's the most northern point on earth, in the middle of the Arctic Ocean. It's not exactly . . . easy to get to. Hence why I require a sleigh and reindeer to get in and out."

"Oh," I say with a heavy sigh, more disappointment coming down over me.

He takes the list off his chest and glances at all the boxes ticked off, all except one, and I can't help but wonder if his mind has gone to the same place mine has. "I'm sorry, Mila," he rumbles. "This list was never intended to break your heart."

"I know. I'm the one who should be sorry," I tell him. "I shouldn't have made a wish for something I knew we could never have. It's just, being away from you for so long, I start to think that maybe things could be different."

"I . . ." he lets out a breath as he sits up, devastation flashing in his eyes. "I'm sorry, I have to go, Mila. Your wishes are complete, and I've been here much longer than I should be allowed."

I suck in a breath, flying to my feet as the sheer panic begins to settle in. "How can it already be time? You've barely been here a few hours," I say, but as my gaze shoots to the window, I realize the sun has already lightened the horizon.

Nick gets up, his eyes softening as he steps into me, his hands finding my waist. "I'm sorry, Mila."

"No. No, no, no. This can't be it already. I only just got you back. I . . . I—"

Nick pulls me in against his chest, holding me tight, his arm curled around my body and his hand in my hair. I cry against his warm chest, listening to the steady beat of his heart—a heart I fear I won't get the chance to see again. What if this is goodbye? What if something happens during the year and one of us realizes it's time to move on? He promises it won't happen, that I'll always be it for him, that when a soul finds its person, it sticks. But how can that truly be real? How can I hold onto this love from someone who I only ever see once a year? He'll soon enough forget me the moment he meets someone new, someone not so far away, someone far less complicated than me.

"Don't," he says. "I know where your head has gone. This isn't it, Mila. I'll come back for you again. Wish me here, just like you did this year."

I pull back, hating the tears staining my cheeks, and as I look up into those dark eyes, I see the same pain in my heart reflected in his eyes. He wants to stay just as much as I need him to, but how am I ever supposed to make this work?

He's going to walk away and my heart will tear to shreds.

Nick takes my hand and leads me out into my living room where he reluctantly gets dressed. He pulls his red coat back on and fixes the belt into place before stepping into his black boots. He's the perfect sexy Santa, and despite having sat with his identity for a year now, it's still crazy to try and wrap my head around.

The moment he's dressed, he takes my hand again, and we make our way to the living room window, just as we had last time. He helps me out onto the fire escape, only this time, the walk up to the roof is silent and filled with deep sorrow. I can't keep the tears from coming, knowing just how hard a year without him truly is.

Reaching the roof, I'm met with the sight of the beautiful reindeer, and just like last December, they completely blow me away. The sleigh is a crazy sight, but the reindeer are what truly hold my attention. We walk toward them, and with each of them awake and ready for their trek back home, I can't help but notice how I hold their attention.

Nick stops just shy of the reindeer, and as he turns to meet my stare, there's a strange reluctance in his eyes, something dark, but I can't quite put my finger on why. "This is really it?" I ask.

He nods. "I'm sorry I couldn't give you all of your wishes."

"I know," I murmur, stepping into him again and feeling the way his strong arms wrap around me. "You don't need to be sorry. I understand. I shouldn't have asked for it. I just . . . I so badly wish that I could be yours. To be with you every day. To have this every day."

That strange darkness flashes in his eyes again. "You don't understand what you're asking for," he says. "Do you know what a life with me would mean?"

"No," I admit. "But I don't even care. I want it. Anything is better than the life I have here without you."

Nick takes a breath, and he looks at me like he's truly struggling to walk away and leave me here broken just as he did last year. His hands ball into tight fists, his jaw clenching and unclenching. He closes his eyes again, and when he opens them, they're somehow even darker. Something within his stare warns me it's time to walk away, but I can't.

"Let me hear you wish it," he murmurs, the pain clear in his deep tone.

I let out a sigh, my hand falling to his and holding it tight, realizing he needs to hear the words just as much as I do. To know that when he leaves, my heart will still belong to him, and with that, I step in even closer and tilt my chin up. "Nick, I wish to be only yours. I wish to fully belong to you, to have your heart every single day of the rest of our lives. I wish to be where you are and start a life with you."

"Are you sure?" he rumbles, his jaw clenching again as his eyes flicker with that terrifying darkness.

"Yes, Nick," I say, willing him to truly hear me. "I've never been so sure. I'm crazy in love with you, and I never want to be away from you like this again. I'm yours, Nick. And I will spend every day of the rest of my life wishing things could be different."

And not a moment later, his hand comes up around the back of my neck, and everything goes black.

CHAPTER 12

NICK

Ahh fuck.

There's messed up and then there is the needs-to-be-imprisoned messed up.

The sleigh touches down on the snow a mile outside of my home, far away from the workshop or where I'm supposed to land, but considering Mila is passed out cold beside me, perhaps showing up within civilization probably isn't the best idea.

I fucking kidnapped her.

What the fuck is wrong with me? She wished for it, and while I still possessed the ability to make her wish come true, I made it happen, but she told me this is what she wanted, so I'm sure once she wakes and realizes what the fuck just went down, she'll be fine with it.

I hope.

Knocking her out though, it was a cold move, but I had no choice. Time was running out. Once the sun broke the horizon on Christmas morning, my ability to grant Christmas wishes diminished. She wouldn't have survived the ride back to the North Pole, so I did what was necessary, even if actually doing it made me fucking sick to my stomach.

I could just see the judgment in the reindeers' eyes. They're gentle beasts, and knocking a girl out clearly didn't sit well with them. They protested the whole way home, making for one hell of a rocky ride, but once they realized I was fucking things up again and not taking them straight back to the main city, they were fucking pissed and they made sure I knew it.

The reindeer are creatures of habit. They like things done a certain way, and when you're the one responsible for fucking with their schedule, they can be absolute assholes. But considering I'm the one who has cared for them most of their lives, I like to believe they'll quickly forgive me. At least when they realize that I'm the one who's going to bring them their dinner, they'll come racing back. These little fuckers like to eat.

The plan today is to . . . fuck. I don't really know. For now, I just want to get her back to my place before she wakes up and realizes what I've done, and after that, I'll work it out as I go.

My brain is a fog of what-ifs.

What if this isn't what she actually wanted?

What if my father figures it out?

What if a life with me isn't actually fulfilling for her?

The questions plague me, one after another, and it's enough to drive me insane as the reindeer race through the snow, taking us the last few feet toward my home. They know exactly where they're going, and as Tucker leads them right to my door, the unease in my chest only gets worse.

The sleigh comes to a stop in the early light of Christmas morning, and as Mila sleeps soundly beside me, I scoop her into my arms, realizing I'm going to have to find my way back to her apartment and pack up her things or have my helpers go out and purchase her a whole new wardrobe. Though to be honest, I've never lived with a woman. I don't really know what she will need. Once she's awake and on board with her whole kidnapping, perhaps we could work it out together.

With Mila securely in my arms, I jump down from the sleigh and walk up the line of reindeer until I reach Tuck at the front. I make sure to scratch him under the chin while doing everything I can to ignore the judgment in his eyes. "Keep your mouth shut about this, and there'll be extra dessert for the next week and a half."

Naturally, the fucker can't talk, but the way he looks at me is almost as though he can perfectly understand what I'm saying, and the slight nod he gives of approval is exactly what I need.

I laugh to myself as I step around him and make my way down the small path that leads toward my front door. It's a short walk, but with Mila in my arms, I'd happily walk the whole fucking globe. I reach my door in no time, and I have to juggle her a bit to get the door open, but I don't have to bother with a key. We don't need to lock our doors around here. The only person who might be a threat when it comes to breaking into other people's homes is probably me.

Sue me. I'm not exactly a great guy, and the fact that I've just kidnapped Mila is more than proof of that.

Taking her into my home is somewhat surreal. I've always dreamed of what it would be like to have her here. Sure, it might not have been under these circumstances, but she made the wish, and I did nothing but grant it. It's my Santa-ly duties after all. Besides, I'd granted the rest of her wishes through the night. Why would she think for even one second that I wouldn't grant that one? You know, apart from the fact I told her I couldn't. I can guarantee that kidnapping really isn't what she had in mind though.

Oh well, she's here now, and considering it's officially sunrise on Christmas morning, there's not a damn thing I can do about it.

Making my way through my home, I use my hip to push open my bedroom door and lay Mila down with her head against my pillow. I pull the snow-white sheets over her shoulders before adding a thick blanket. I have heating here, but the freezing temperature outside always wins, no matter how hard I run the heating.

I want to be here when Mila wakes, but if I don't circle back and return the sleigh for its usual Christmas Day maintenance, my father is bound to come asking questions, and finding Mila out cold in my bed isn't the way I want to break the news that their only son kidnapped a woman during the night.

Mila is well and truly out, and considering the long night we've both had, I can only assume she'll be out for a few more hours. So with that resolve, I leave her be, closing the door behind me as I walk out of the bedroom. In a perfect world, I'd lie down beside her and spend all day sleeping with her in my arms, but duty calls, and unfortunately, I don't have the luxury of calling the shots right now.

Making my way out of my home, I pull the front door closed, and just as I'm walking back to the sleigh, I hesitate. Leaving the door unsecured feels like a bad idea this time, so I double back to lock it. I know I just said that we don't have to worry about that around here, but in this particular case, I'm trying to keep someone from breaking out rather than breaking in.

If Mila wakes up when I'm not here, I don't want to risk her taking off. My home is surrounded by a reindeer farm, and outside of that is a thick line of woods. I don't want to risk her freaking out and running, only to get her ass lost in the woods. Don't get me wrong, I'd spend the rest of my life searching for her out there if I had to, but Mila strikes me as the type to run first and think later, and considering her lack of clothing, that could be an issue.

With that all sorted and Mila tucked safely in my bed, I take off, more than ready to drop these reindeer and the sleigh off, debrief after my run, and check in on my parents before finally making my way back here to face Mila's wrath.

CHAPTER 13

MILA

A strange woodsy scent hits my nose, and just as consciousness begins to come back to me, I slowly peel my eyes open to a strange room. What the actual fuck happened?

I try to look around, and the moment my eyes shift inside my head, an instant headache booms inside my skull like a million tiny little Christmas elves have crawled in through my ears, set up a million little drum sets, and spent the night raving inside my skull. I immediately close my eyes again, willing the pain to subside.

Maybe if I stay as still as possible and keep my eyes closed, the darkness behind my lids will eventually trick my brain into thinking my headache has faded. Though I've never been that lucky when it comes to shit like this. A good migraine can usually take me out for days.

Perhaps I'm in the hospital. Last thing I knew, I was standing on the roof with Nick, desperately wishing he could stay, and the next, I was out cold.

Perhaps something happened with one of the reindeer and they accidentally knocked me out. Maybe I got too close to the sleigh on takeoff and hit my head, erasing the few minutes of memory beforehand. Either way, whatever happened, I'm pissed. I've lost my final goodbye with Nick, and now I'm going to have to wait another whole year before I get to see him again.

After a few minutes, I finally risk opening my eyes again, expecting to see the clinical walls of a hospital room. Instead, I find myself tucked into a huge king-sized bed, the pillows softer than anything I've ever felt in my life. The white feather blankets feel as though they were handcrafted by angels and sent straight from heaven.

"What in the ever-loving fuck?"

I push up onto my elbow. Don't get me wrong, this bed is simply divine, but how the fuck did I get into it? And more importantly, who put me into it? Because the one thing I know for sure is that this is certainly no hospital room. No subtle beep on a heart rate monitor. No nurses walking by the door. No stiff, itchy blankets.

I look closer.

The room I'm in seems more like someone's personal bedroom, and yet, also so far from that. There's nothing in here that suggests it belongs to anyone. No pictures around the room, no hint of personal style, and no personal belongings left scattered on the bedside table. In my shitty apartment, you can't walk an inch without seeing something of mine strewn across the room. Pictures of my parents in frames or clothes left hanging over the back of the couch. This room though, it's the complete opposite.

My heart races as I get the feeling something isn't right here, and I sit up fully before throwing the blankets right back and immediately regretting it. It's fucking freezing.

My nipples harden for all the wrong reasons, and I hastily wrap my arms around myself as I stumble out of the bed. I'm still wearing the silk gown I was wearing on the rooftop with Nick, so I guess that's a positive that nobody has attempted to take it off me. However, it's not as though I was wearing anything beneath it. I'm naked under this thin piece of material, and that's not exactly offering me a lot of confidence.

Just how long have I been passed out? And more importantly, has someone taken advantage of me while I wasn't able to defend myself?

I try to take stock of my body, feeling around to make sure everything is as it should be. Everything is sore, and yet after the wild night I just spent with Nick, it's impossible to tell if that's him I'm still feeling or if something a little more sinister is going on.

I begin padding around the room with my arms locked protectively around my body, trying to keep warm, but with every single step, it becomes even more clear that something is off here. My heart races faster, and unease pulses through my veins as I pause in front of the huge window in the bedroom.

"Holy fucking shit."

The view of New York City I expected has changed. Instead of city lights over slushy streets, I find myself looking out at an expanse of snowcapped hills. There are reindeer everywhere, completely unaware of the way I'm starting to freak out.

Reindeer could only mean one thing.

This is all Nick's doing.

He brought me here. He's responsible for . . . whatever the fuck this is. It's clear as day I'm no longer in New York, but what about the United States? Am I still in the country I was raised in and have called home for the past twenty-seven years?

Holy shit. This is not happening. I wasn't knocked out by accident. Nick did this.

I know I asked to be with him, to be his, but I never realized that meant having my world stripped away. Sure. the life I had in New York wasn't amazing. I was miserable most of the time, but it was mine. I created it and despite everything, I was proud of what little I'd accomplished on my own and now ... it's just gone. New York is the resting place of my parents. It's where I grew up, where I went to school, and had my first kiss. It's my home, and in a matter of seconds, it was stripped away from me. I didn't even get a chance to say goodbye.

What have I done?

Horror begins pounding at my chest, and I hastily move around the room, finding a bathroom and then a huge walk-in closet. It's like nothing I've ever seen, and yet every piece of clothing inside is either black or Santa Claus red.

Fuck. Fuck. Fuck. Fuck. Fuck.

With the cold threatening to take me out, I have no choice but to grab one of Nick's oversized hoodies and a pair of sweatpants. I quickly pull them on, not exactly thrilled about the way the material swims on me, but it's all I've got to work with right now. Searching through drawers, I find some socks and a pair of boots before dropping down to my ass to pull them on.

The socks are everything I never knew I needed, and in my panic of realizing Nick has potentially kidnapped me, I hadn't even realized just how frozen my feet had become. But these socks . . . shit. They're just like the blanket on the bed, hand-crafted specifically for my warmth.

After pulling on the boots, I get to my feet. I'm not exactly thrilled about their fit either. Nick is huge, and naturally, so are his boots, but if I plan on surviving the weather out there, I'm going to need something a little sturdier than my silk gown to keep me warm.

With equal parts determination and anxiety, I make my way to the bedroom door, more than ready to face whatever stands in my way. Only as I reach for the door handle, I pause.

I hadn't exactly thought about what lies on the other side of this door, but now that I'm standing here, ready to barge through it, I'm not quite feeling so confident. What if Nick is standing on the other side waiting for me? What if it's not Nick at all? What if I'm about to be faced with something horrible?

Fuck me. How did I get myself into this situation?

I should have known better. When the mystery guy who visited me every Christmas Eve admitted that he has some slight stalker tendencies, I should have seen that as a blazing red flag. However, I've been so deprived of love and affection, so desperate to feel something, that I didn't even notice how fucked up it was. All that mattered was how good the sex was, how fast my heart raced around him, and how quickly Christmas would come around again. I was all for it. Ready to hand myself over to a fucking psychopath.

What the fuck is wrong with me? Why do I keep ending up with men who are batshit crazy? Though to be fair to my ex, he wasn't crazy. He was just an asshole. But apparently, Nick is too. I should have heeded his warnings when he said he was the black sheep of the family. He told me point-blank that he was an asshole, that the people who know him tolerate him out of fear, and all I did was bat my fucking eyelashes at the guy and beg him to take me again.

If I ever make it out of here, I should see to it that I'm committed, straitjacket and all.

Realizing there's no time quite like the present, I try to ignore the nerves infecting my body and slowly begin to open the bedroom door. The house seems too silent, and I find myself holding my breath and listening to every little noise as the door inches open.

It doesn't sound like there's anyone here, and as the door opens just enough for me to peek through the gap, I take a hasty look around, making sure no little whore elves are about to jump out at me. Nick said there were no elves, but honestly, that really shattered my illusion of Christmas. I was all for the whore elves.

Positive that I'm alone, I pull the door all the way open and slowly step out into the main part of the house.

It's fucking massive.

No one on this green earth needs a home this fucking big, but hell, if anyone would, why wouldn't it be the Grinch who masquerades as jolly old Saint Nick?

Fucking asshole.

Did he really kidnap me? Knock me out and shove my ass into his big red sleigh only to bring me here . . . wherever that may be. The North Pole, I'm assuming. The place he told me was almost impossible to get to.

Shit, I'm well and truly fucked.

I can barely wrap my head around it, and as I step out of the bedroom with my massive boots, I search for a way to free myself from this hell hole. Okay, I mean, it's not actually a hell hole. This home is magnificent. I would happily live here any day of the week, but the fact that Nick has brought me here without my consent automatically makes me hate it.

Shit. Why didn't I listen when he said he was an asshole? I've been so blinded by my rampant feelings for him that I couldn't see what was right in front of my face. Even now, knowing what he's done, my heart still races at the thought of getting to see him. Though, if I don't get my stupid ass out of here soon, seeing him again is probably going to come a shitload sooner than I originally anticipated.

Making my way around the room, I cross through the massive living space, and assuming I'm here for the rest of my life, I can tell I'm going to spend a decent amount of time on that couch. It looks good enough to live on, but for now, I must concentrate.

I don't even bother to make my way into the massive kitchen, instead, I cross right to the foyer and hurry to the front door, only as I grab it and start to twist, I come up short. The fucker is locked.

"Shit."

Panic begins to rise in my chest, and I hastily whip around, my gaze jumping around the extraordinary home, searching for a way out. There are windows everywhere, and as I race around the house, I realize that every single one of them has been locked as well.

What kind of psychopath locks every single window? Everyone knows that you always leave one open for those days you lock yourself out of your house and you've forgotten where you hid the spare key. Or is that just a me thing?

After a thorough check of the house, I realize there isn't a single way out, and I start to get fidgety, not enjoying this one bit. How the hell am I supposed to stage my grand escape when I can't even get through the door? Damn it. If this was a horror movie, I'd be the first one killed, and what's worse, I'd probably insist that my would-be murderer fuck me up against the wall first and make me a replica of his dick for me to ride until I get to see him again.

Figuring my only hope now is to escape through a broken window, I go in search of something I can use to smash the glass, but all I come up with is the armchair in the living room. I don't exactly have much of a plan after that. Nick mentioned that there are a bunch of helpers here, and I'm assuming his parents too, who I really hope are nice people and would be able to help me. If I find them, perhaps I'm one step closer to finding my way back home.

Taking the armchair, I test its weight, seeing just how far I might be able to throw it, but I pause when I hear the front door unlocking.

The door opens with speed, not allowing me a chance to even run and hide, and within seconds, Nick's dark gaze is locked on mine.

"Ahh fuck," he mutters, cringing as he eyes the chair above my head. "I was hoping you'd still be out cold."

What in the actual fuck is wrong with this guy?

I can't respond. Is he seriously that insane?

Nick creeps toward me, and seeing the way I stare back at him like a deer in headlights, he holds his hands out as if to try and soothe me and ensure he means no harm. But fuck, I've fallen for his bullshit before.

As he takes another step, my fight-or-flight instincts kick in, and I finally find my voice. "Don't come any closer," I snap, tightening my hold on the armchair, positive that at some point it will probably throw me off balance.

"Woah, baby," he says. "It's okay. I'm not going to hurt you. Put the chair down."

"Are you fucking insane?"

He shrugs his shoulders as if he's actually considering it. "I've never been tested, but . . ."

He lets his comment fall away, leaving me gaping at him. "What the fuck is going on, Nick? Where the hell am I?"

"This is my home," he says, waving his hands around this massive place.

"Gee, thanks, asshole," I snap, adjusting my stance every time he inches toward me. "I'd figured that much out when I woke up in a fucking snow globe. I meant where am I? Where the hell have you brought me?"

He cringes again, those dark eyes that have haunted every single one of my dreams suddenly the object of my future nightmares. "We're in the North Pole, Mila," he explains. "I simply gave you what you wished for."

"What?" I demand, shaking my head as I finally put the chair down. "No, this isn't—"

"You wished to be mine," he says. "You wished to be with me every day of the rest of our lives. To belong to only me. I gave you what you asked for, Mila. You wanted this, and now you have it. You're mine."

I back up a few steps, my back only inches from hitting the

living room window. "No. That's not what I meant," I say, my heart pounding so hard in my chest, terrified of what I've done—of what he's done. "You knocked me out and stole me away. How the hell could you possibly think that's what I wanted?"

"I told you that you didn't understand what you were asking for, what a life with me would mean, but you said you didn't care. You said anything is better than the life you had in New York without me."

I shake my head as he continues creeping toward me. "I . . . I didn't realize—"

"It's going to be okay," he says, stepping into me, his hands finding my waist, only I spring back, slamming my hands down to knock his touch away.

"Don't," I rush out, darting across the living room and only narrowly avoiding him, yet when he takes another step in my direction, I can't help but grab the small vase off the coffee table and launch it toward his stupidly gorgeous head.

Nick avoids the flying vase with ease and we both watch as it smashes against the wall behind his glorious head. "Really?" he says, his gaze slowly coming back to mine.

"Take me home," I demand, clenching my jaw and mustering up every ounce of defiance I can possibly find within myself. "This isn't what I meant, and you know it. I wanted a life with you, yes. But I wanted a life on my terms. You have literally stolen me away from everything I know."

"You were fucking miserable in New York."

"I DON'T CARE," I yell. "I had the right to decide for myself if I wanted to be swept away. This place is . . ." I look around, not able to find the words to describe Nick's home, but lonely sure comes to mind. "There's not another soul in sight. No other homes, nothing for me to do here but sit and wait and play the role of your perfect little wifey. Well, fuck you. I don't want it like this. Take me home."

Nick clenches his jaw, something shifting in his dark stare. "I can't do that."

"The fuck you can't," I demand. "Take me home. Now."

Nick strides toward me, and this time, I don't flinch away from him, somehow knowing that he won't hurt me. "My hands are tied, Mila. I can't take you home," he tells me, those dark eyes lingering so deeply on mine and confusing every thought inside my head. "You made a Christmas wish, and now that your wishes have been carried out, there's nothing I can do about it. If you truly don't want to be here, then you need to wish it away."

Pain lingers behind his eyes, and for just a moment, I can almost pretend that maybe he really wanted this. Maybe bringing me here wasn't some sinister plan to kidnap me. Maybe everything he did was out of love. But I was right to question myself. How can you love somebody you don't even know?

"Then I wish it away," I tell him, unsure why I feel as though my heart is tearing in two. "I wish to be taken back to New York."

Nick simply stands there, his gaze locked on mine. "You don't truly mean that."

I raise my chin, unsure why my eyes are filling with tears. "I do," I tell him, hating how I wish he would wrap his arms around me and hold me to his chest, telling me that everything is going to be okay.

"I can't grant you something you don't truly desire, Mila," he says, his hand coming up and brushing the side of my face. "I know you are confused and unsure about how all of this has played out, but you don't truly wish to be sent back home. You wanted this. You wanted to be mine."

I shove him away, my emotions in an epic game of ping pong and giving me whiplash. "Yes, I might have wanted to be with you, but not like this," I say, the tears finally flowing free. "Send me home."

He shakes his head. "Like I said, I can't do that."

"You can and you will. That's what I want. What I wished for."

"It's not quite as simple as that," he tells me. "Once the sun rises on Christmas morning, I no longer possess the ability to grant your wishes. Look around you, Mila. The sun has fallen, and Christmas Day is almost over."

My brows furrow as I follow his gaze out the window. "What are you saying? That I'm stuck here?"

Nick nods. "Yes. For the next twelve months. Come next December, if you truly want to leave, all you need to do is wish it."

"Holy fucking shit." I press my hands to my temples as I pace the length of the living room, my headache suddenly coming back in full force. "Twelve fucking months? I'm stuck here in this snow globe prison for a whole year?"

"Surely you must understand," he says. "I have loved you since I was a boy. I was fine watching from the sidelines, but the moment you allowed me to touch you, there was no going back for me. I am yours. I have always been yours."

"Oh wow. Lucky me. My kidnapper is in love. How fucking sweet."

"Mila—"

"You're a psychopath."

Nick grins, and his eyes dance with darkness. "Perhaps. But that's what you like about me, isn't it, baby?" he murmurs, stepping into me again, his dark stare locking onto mine and catching me completely unaware. "You liked it when I snuck into your room every Christmas Eve. You like when you get me so worked up that I have no choice but to fuck myself. And you fucking love it when that wild part of me comes out and makes you scream. Don't start denying that this is exactly what you want. You asked for this. You asked for me, and now that you've got it, you're going to stand here and pretend that this isn't exactly what you've been craving all fucking year."

I shove him away again, only this time he doesn't budge. He simply catches my hands against his chest, the way his heart is racing just as fast as mine almost brings me to my knees. "You took away my right to choose."

"I took away your ability to hide from what you truly wanted," he tells me. "You're scared of wanting something you shouldn't. You're scared of letting yourself actually feel for a change. I gave you what your heart truly desired. So what if I had to kidnap you to make it happen? I won't apologize for that. I get to have you every fucking day now."

I scoff. "You're not having anything."

"So be it, Mila. But just knowing you are here in my home is more than enough for me. I don't need to fuck you to know I still have you."

Yanking my hands free, I tear away from him. "You're a cocky bastard."

"Yes," he agrees. No question about it.

"So, just like that, I'm trapped here for the next twelve months?"

"The North Pole is so much more than the reindeer farm outside the window. Give it a chance, Mila. Despite what you might think, I know your heart, and I think after you truly see what it is we do here, you will fall in love with this place. The next twelve months won't be enough for you, and soon enough, you will start to realize how wrong you were to ever want to go back to your mundane, lonely life in New York. You belong here with me. You just don't know it yet."

CHAPTER 14

MILA

He is legitimately crazy, and a part of me actually believes that he thinks he's done the right thing by kidnapping me. He might not have gotten his rocks off by knocking me out, but having me here in his home is definitely getting him hard.

This is all my fault. I welcomed him into my home every year, wished for him to come, and slowly fell in love with the idea of him. Only when he touched me, everything changed.

Why did I have to fall in love with a guy who has no moral compass? Surely that must make me just as messed up as he is.

I sit in his oversized living room, my knees pulled right up to my chest on the couch that is even more comfortable than it looks, but I'm not about to tell him that. Though, I'm getting a sick sense of satisfaction from the way his eye seems to twitch by me having his big-ass boots propped on the cushion. Seems someone likes his home to be nice and clean. I'll be sure to make a mental note of that and not accidentally make the kind of messes that drive him insane. After all, I wouldn't want to make these next twelve months miserable for the man who literally stole me from my home.

Wish or not, he shouldn't have done it.

"So this is how the next twelve months are going to play out?" Nick asks, circling the back of his dining table and clutching the top of the chair as his gaze remains locked on me.

"Look around you, Nick. Your home is surrounded by reindeer and snow. It's not like there's exactly a lot to do apart from fucking each other, and unfortunately for you, the only thing you'll be fucking is your hand."

"Better than being fucking delusional like you are."

"Delusional?" I demand, but the grin on his face suggests he's saying it just to get a rise out of me, and damn it, it worked like a charm. Refusing to play into his bullshit, I avert my gaze and stare at the reindeer out the window.

Clearly realizing that I'm more than happy to spend the next twelve months ignoring him, Nick lets out a sigh. "I've got shit I need to do. Is there anything you need first?"

Glancing over my shoulder, I offer him a sugary-sweet smile, batting my lashes and watching the way his whole body seems to soften. "Only for you to pull out the knife currently in my back, sweetheart."

His face falls, and I can't help but wonder if he thought for just a moment that I'd actually started to come around. But surely he knows better than that.

I watch as he finally gives in, realizing that I'm not about to break. He lets out a subtle sigh, and with that, he disappears into his bedroom . . . our bedroom.

A minute passes, and I hear Nick undressing. It's a sound already so familiar to me, and within seconds, I get lost in the memory of what it's like every time he undresses around me. He might have asshole tendencies, but when it comes to giving me exactly what I need, he's never let me down.

Hunger blooms through my chest, and for just a moment, I consider putting my frustration aside and barging through the bedroom door to have my wicked way with him. I doubt he'll have any issues with it. If anything, he'll give it to me a little harder just because I've been acting like a brat, but he's not about to get to me that easily. What he might not know about me is when I've been wronged, I'm a stubborn bitch until I feel justice has been served, and in this case, justice hasn't even begun to be served.

Doing what I can to try and calm the raging need within me, I suddenly realize this is my one shot to slip away, and in the blink of an eye, I'm on my feet, darting to the front door, more than ready to make my hasty escape.

I all but lunge for the door handle, gripping it hard and violently twisting, only to be met with nothing. The door doesn't move, the handle not even budging an inch, and I curse myself for being such an idiot. Of course the big asshole locked it again.

Damn it.

I pace through the foyer, trying to figure out a game plan when my gaze comes back to the armchair that was once angled nicely in the corner of the living room. Only now it's half knocked over, leaning up against the couch from my earlier woman-handling.

I hurry toward it. This is definitely a bad idea, but what choice do I have? The second I throw the chair through the window, I'll only have a moment to get away before Nick comes racing after me. I'm a pretty good runner. I spent a lot of time in the gym this year trying to pass the time. I could run for miles before passing out, but Nick is fit too, and judging by the ruthless way he fucks, I don't doubt he could chase me for hours. All I need is to get far enough away to find another living soul, and I'll be good.

Not ready to give up on the one shot I have, I go for it, grabbing the chair and launching it toward the massive window with every bit of strength I possess.

The chair plunges through the glass, and the noise is deafening as it shatters into a million fractured pieces.

"FUCK! MILA," I hear Nick calling from the bedroom, but I'm already gone, racing through what was once a beautiful window until my too-big boots come crashing down into the snow.

I put one foot in front of the other, not daring to look back as I run toward the reindeer farm. My arms pump on either side of me, taking me as fast as I can go. I'm not exactly a great sprinter, but I'll manage a steady run with no problem.

As I reach the edge of the reindeer farm, I realize just how high the fences are, and knowing damn well I won't be able to launch myself over it, I have no choice but to shift to the right, taking myself around the edges and toward the woods beyond. If I can reach the thick trees, I'll be able to make my way along the tree line until I finally find some sign of life. Surely this place has got to have some kind of city, right? Or at the very least, a small town.

The thick snow beneath my feet slows me down, but I don't dare stop, especially when I hear Nick somewhere in the distance. "MILA, WHERE ARE YOU?"

Shit. Shit. Shit.

I definitely didn't think this through, especially considering he'll have no problem tracking me through the massive footprints left in the snow. Not to mention, he's lived here his whole life. He knows these woods, and he sure as fuck has a lot more practice moving around in the snow than I ever could.

My lungs scream for air, but I don't dare stop as I quickly approach the trees, and the second I break through the foliage, I dart behind a thick trunk and lean my head back against the bark, taking deep breaths as I try to figure out my next plan of attack.

I give myself just a moment to catch my breath before finally allowing myself to look back around the trunk. I see Nick in the distance, quickly eating up the space between us, and as my gaze drops to the snow, I see the obvious tracks I've made.

Fuck. There's no escaping him like this.

"YOU CAN'T RUN FROM ME, BABY."

I scoff. Wanna bet?

Taking a risk, I lunge out from behind the tree, and with what few precious seconds I have left, I race through the snow, going left and right, back and forth, quickly dissolving my tracks, and just as Nick approaches the tree line, I dart behind the thick trunk once again.

I hear his footsteps as he comes to a stop, and I slam my hand over my mouth, trying to control my deep breathing. It won't be long before he finds me. I have to get going.

"Come on, Mila. I know you're here," he says, his voice so low, it does wicked things to me. "I'm going to find you, and when I do, I'm going to fuck that attitude right out of you."

Good God. My pussy spasms, and I clench my thighs, suddenly so hungry for him.

What the fuck is wrong with me? I suppose when the sex is good, a woman is willing to ignore every red flag, even when they're flying right in front of her face.

I follow the sound of his footsteps and when he begins walking in the opposite direction, I can't help but peer around the tree once again, only this time, everything stops. Nick didn't bother dressing before he raced after me, and all I see is this beast of a man, his perfect ass and chiseled back staring back at me. He's wearing nothing but a pair of undone boots with his hand covering his junk, and fuck, he looks glorious.

The hunger intensifies, and I watch every step he takes, so damn focused on the way his muscled back moves. He's simply divine. No wonder I haven't been able to resist him. He's the absolute definition of perfection.

What the fuck am I doing running away from this? It's not as though I had the best life back home in New York. I was on the verge of depression. I hate my job, hate my apartment, and what's worse, I haven't got a single person in my life I'm able to call friend. And yet, here's Nick, offering me everything I've ever wanted, and I'm literally running away from it. Sure, he went about it in the most fucked-up way possible, which he will be punished for. But why should I have to punish myself for his actions too? Surely if I'm going to be the victim of his schemes, I should at least get something out of it, right?

Would it be so terrible if I stayed the twelve months? I could spend them in Nick's bed, making the most of our time together before he finally sends me back home. Sure, it's pure insanity, but if I have to be here, I might as well enjoy it.

"I will find you, Mila. And I will take you."

Fuck. This is probably the most moronic thing I'll ever do.

Pulling my arms inside the oversized hoodie, I slip it over my head before hanging it off a low-lying branch and immediately regretting it as I feel the chill against my skin. But that doesn't stop me, and the next thing I know, I'm letting Nick's sweatpants fall off my hips to the snowy ground. I brace myself against the tree as I work my foot out of the boot and move the sweatpants, only to shove my foot back into the boot. I do the same on the other side until I'm just as naked as Nick is, everything except the boots.

And with that, I step out from behind the tree, coming face to face with jolly old Saint Nick. "Hey Santa Claus," I purr, watching as his gaze flicks up to meet mine. "If you want me, you're gonna have to catch me first."

His jaw clenches, his eyes darkening by the second, and I watch as his cock quickly comes alive, going from being covered to fisted in the blink of an eye. And damn it, he makes me so wet.

There's a wicked look in his eye that warns me I have no idea what I just got myself into, but he should know better by now. Anything he's willing to put down, I'm more than happy to pick up.

Then in a flash, he storms after me, and a high-pitched squeal of laughter tears from the back of my throat. I spin on my heel and leap into the snow, my heavy boots taking me further into the woods.

Hearing Nick race after me makes my heart pound, but I don't let up. If he wants me, he's going to work for it. I hear his footsteps behind me, and just as I risk glancing back, my boot catches on a stray tree root, and I crash down in the snow, my knees hitting the cold ground as my face and tits slam against the snow, leaving my ass and cunt high in the air for Nick to claim anyway he sees fit.

"Mmmm, baby," he growls, and fuck, I can only imagine how I

look to him right now. I can't resist looking back over my shoulder, finding him standing right behind me, his chest heaving just like mine is as he grips that massive cock, slowly pumping his fist up and down.

My pussy clenches, and I have no doubt that he can see just how wet I am for him. "Fuck me, Nick," I beg him. "And you better make it good because it's the last one you'll get."

He clenches his jaw again, something shifting in his dark eyes, and not a moment later, he drops down behind me in the snow. Both of our knees are at risk of frostbite, but I couldn't give a single fuck. His free hand rests against my ass.

"You broke my window," he murmurs, his palm slowly brushing over my ass cheek before shifting to my center.

I push back against his touch, desperate for him to slam inside of me and relieve the ache he's given me. "Seems like it's a fair trade considering you broke my heart."

"I didn't break your heart, Mila," he says, finally pushing two thick fingers deep inside of me, curving them just right and driving me wild in seconds. "You're doing that all on your own."

He fucks me with his fingers, and I keep pushing back, desperate for relief. He might be right. I might be breaking my own heart, but right now, I couldn't seem to care less. All that matters is feeling him inside of me. "Nick," I groan. "Fuck me."

"Patience, Mila."

His fingers keep working me, massaging inside of me, rolling and splitting, until my walls begin shaking around his fingers. He pushes me further, stretching his thumb toward my clit and applying just enough pressure to set me alight. Even in this freezing snow, all I feel is the heat from my core.

"NICK!"

"Come for me, Mila. Give me what's mine."

I fall to pieces, shattering just like the glass I broke in his living room, and with every roll of his fingers inside of me, my orgasm intensifies. My toes curl inside my boots as I shamelessly grab at the snow-covered ground.

"Oh. Fuck. Nick. YES!"

His thumb works my clit, and just as I start coming down from my high, he pulls his fingers free, giving me just a moment of ease before I feel his raging tip at my entrance. "Mmm I'm going to enjoy you, my sweet snow bunny. I'm going to take this sweet cunt, and by the time I'm done with you, that attitude of yours better be fucked out of your system, and if it's not, I'm going to fuck that pretty mouth until it is. Do you understand me?"

I swallow the nerves, my nipples painfully hard against the snow, and I nod. "Between you and me, Nick. I'm the one who should be making demands. Now slam that thick cock inside of me and let me scream."

He doesn't hesitate, giving me exactly what I asked for, his fingers digging into my hip.

I push back against him, taking him as deep as I possibly can as he slams into me over and over again, his balls grinding against my clit. It's too much, yet not nearly enough, and I can't help but reach beneath me until my fingers are stroking either side of my entrance as he works my cunt. I feel the way he fucks me, the way he thrusts into me, and within seconds, my thighs are shaking.

"Fuck, Nick," I groan, snow plastered to the side of my face.

He grunts in response, and I lower my fingers to my clit, rubbing greedy circles, this time not caring if it's a long game or a fast one. Though to be honest, I don't know if I can last much longer with my knees in the freezing snow. It's starting to burn, but it's a pain I'd happily endure, especially considering this will be the last time he ever gets to fuck me. In theory, of course. Who knows how weak I'll be over the next year.

Pushing my knees further apart, Nick takes me deeper, and I cry out again, the raw power of his thrusts more than fucking the attitude out of me, and damn it, if this is what I get for being a bitch, I might have to show him just how bitchy I can truly be.

He rolls his hips and takes me at a whole new angle, and I feel the familiar sensation building within me, intense and raw, more than ready to send me into an abyss of sweet pleasure. I pick up my pace, rolling circles over my clit just a little bit faster, and he immediately picks up on my need, thrusting deeper and harder, giving me exactly what I need to get me there, and not a moment later, I come hard, my whole universe shaking beneath me.

I fall to pieces as he continues to fuck me, not letting up until

I've reached my high and started to come back down. "How's that attitude, baby?" he rumbles, his fingers digging deeper into my flesh, warning me just how close he really is.

"Just as strong as ever," I tell him, not nearly over his kidnapping antics.

A deep groan rumbles through his chest, and before I know it, Nick pulls himself free and flips me over, my back coming down against the freezing snow. I arch up off the cold with a hiss, but Nick comes down over me, straddling my chest and keeping me pinned beneath him. He grips his thick cock, those dark eyes like lasers on mine. "What did I tell you, Mila?"

I shake my head, having no fucking idea. I'm still buried deep in my post-orgasm fog, I barely know what's happening.

"I warned you what would happen if that attitude wasn't fucked out of you."

Well damn. That particular little speech might be coming back.

"Remember?"

I nod.

"What did I tell you would happen?"

My tongue rolls over my bottom lip. "You'd fuck my pretty mouth."

"Open."

I narrow my gaze, the hunger rapidly building again, but that doesn't mean I'm going to make it easy for him. "I hope you don't mind teeth," I say, and as his brow arches with alarm, I open wide and take him deep in my throat.

It's awkward having to lift my neck to be able to take him, but I wiggle my arm free and fist the bottom of his cock, working him with my mouth, tongue, and hand at the same time. He grits his teeth and just when he thinks he's got it easy, I roll my tongue over his tip and watch the hunger flash in his eyes.

His hips jolt forward, forcing him deeper down my throat, and I welcome every inch. Despite everything, I'm still more than willing to please him. On my terms of course, which is exactly where my teeth come into play.

I narrow my jaw, my teeth gently coming down along his shaft as I move up and down his velvety cock. He sucks in a breath, his hand falling on top of mine at his base as though that could somehow control my movements. He doesn't know whether to fear for his manhood or to relax and enjoy whatever brutal pleasure I have in store for him, but meeting my stare, he chooses to trust me, allowing me to continue, and that's exactly what I do.

My tongue doesn't let up, rolling over his sensitive tip before I move back down his length, letting my teeth tease as I continue to suck, taking him as far down my throat as I can tolerate. His eyes begin to flutter, rolling in the back of his head as his hips grow a mind of their own, continuously bucking toward me.

He reaches back, his fingers slipping between my thighs and rolling over my needy clit, and as I work him to the edge, he does the same for me. I push and push, giving him my absolute best work, watching closely as he begins to fall apart, completely at my mercy.

"Fuck, Mila," he grits through his clenched teeth, and all I can do is grin against his delicious cock. I don't give in, just keep working him harder and faster until he can't take it a second longer and explodes hot spurts of cum into the back of my throat as he roars my name.

I come with him, my orgasm tearing through my body as he empties himself. I cry out around his cock, my whole body squirming beneath him, my hips bucking with desperation. Then finally, when he's got nothing left to give, he slowly pulls out of my mouth, and I make a show of licking my lips as he softens his hand against my core, allowing me the chance to relax.

Nick falls to the snow, pulling me with him so that my back no longer burns against the cold, and he simply holds me on his chest, the sound of his heart so perfectly in sync with mine as we catch our breath.

"I don't know how to hate you," I tell him, my hand resting against his chest beside my face.

"Then don't," he wills, dropping his palm to my ass and making small circles.

I let out a heavy breath, wishing I could somehow just let it go, but I'm far too stubborn for that. "It's not that easy," I tell him. "It's going to take some time."

"I know," he says. "But all I ask is that you try. I know this isn't how you wanted any of this to happen, but I was running out of time and did what I had to do. If I had waited another minute, the sun would have risen, and I would have been gone another year. I couldn't bear to leave you behind. Not again."

I simply nod, not knowing how to respond until he finally sits us up. "Come on," he murmurs, brushing my hair back off my face. "Let's get you out of the cold, and then you can ignore me while I cook you dinner."

My stomach grumbles at the thought of a good home-cooked meal, and I realize that I haven't eaten in well over twenty-four hours. "Okay," I tell him. "But just so you know, when I commit to ignoring someone, I really commit."

"I wouldn't expect anything less," he says, and with that, he scoops me out of the snow and starts making the trek back, heading past the curious reindeer and finally through the brand-new side entrance, courtesy of the pretty beige armchair laying in the snow.

CHAPTER 15

NICK

<u>FEBRUARY</u>

There's no doubt about it. When Mila Morgan commits to something, she really fucking commits. We're six weeks into the year and seven weeks into our new living arrangement and not a single fucking word has come out of her devilish mouth.

We've quickly learned how to be around each other without communication. Well, at least one of us attempts to communicate while the other pretends she isn't listening. Sure, I understand why she's doing it. She wants to punish me for stealing her away from the life she had in New York, but I'm not sorry. The moment she finally decides to give this place a real chance, she'll understand why I did it.

Mila Morgan belongs here. She belongs with me, and despite what she might think right now, she is mine and I am hers.

Our days pretty much consist of Mila pretending she's asleep when I get up to work. Only, joke's on her because most nights I stay up watching her sleep, and the moment she's in a deep sleep, she'll roll right into my arms and stay there all night.

I head off to work, figuring out all the ins and outs for the new year of gift giving while Mila spends her days with the reindeer. She didn't come right out and ask, but she wanted to know how to care for them, so I showed her exactly what to do, and she loves it. Every day there's a smile on her face, but it doesn't go unnoticed that the only thing she won't do is muck out the stalls. She leaves all that shit for me to deal with. Fair enough, though. I didn't ask her to take on that responsibility. She does it because she wants to.

The moment I get home, I make dinner and watch the way she watches me, all while she's pretending not to even notice me in the house. She's learned my routine. When I prefer to eat. What foods I like, right down to what time of day I like to shower. It also doesn't go unnoticed that every time I finish in the shower and walk into my walk-in closet to dress, she's always right there, sitting on our bed as though she doesn't possibly have anything else to do. And the second my towel disappears, her eyes are only for me.

Every day is the same, and despite how she still refuses to talk to me, I sense her peace. She likes it here, and I like having her here. I like her in my space. I like her in my home. In my bed. But most of all, I like just being able to see her every fucking day. I've gone from years of craving her to getting her every day, even if all she has to offer is to unintentionally hold me while she sleeps.

APRIL

Grabbing my shit, I go to leave for the day and come to a standstill as I find Mila blocking my exit. She's usually out with the reindeer every morning, and when I leave, I watch her out in the field as she teaches them how to trust her.

I won't lie, I'm starting to get really fucking jealous of the attention she gives them. I'd give anything to see her smile at me the way she smiles at them, but beggars can't be choosers, and she'll eventually come around. She just needs to understand it first. It might have been a selfish act for me to bring her here, but I was granting her wish and giving her exactly what she wanted. If only she realized that. She's too busy blaming me and too fucking stubborn to see that I was doing exactly what she asked. I guess that's exactly what I love about her.

"You need something?" I ask, not bothering to try and figure it out this time. Usually she just stares at me until I make suggestions about what she could possibly need, but not today. I haven't heard her voice in four fucking months, and it's killing me.

Mila just stares, but I can play this game a lot longer than she can. She's got no idea what stubborn really means, and she's playing with the fucking master.

She glances away, not willing to meet my stare, and I step right into her, watching as she sucks in a breath. Her hands twitch at her sides as if physically restraining herself from reaching out and touching me. "What do you need, Mila?"

She visibly swallows, her bright green gaze lifting to mine once again, her chin tilted with defiance. She hesitates, wanting to ask for something, but she's too stubborn to open her damn mouth. So instead, I go to step around her. If she wants something, she can be the one to break.

"Have a good day," I tell her, before walking down the path.

"Fuck," I hear behind me, the sweet tone of her voice bringing me to a stop. "Nick. Wait."

I whip around, my brow arched, and I wait patiently for her to continue, but the words get stuck in her throat as she wars with her inner demons.

A soft smile pulls at my lips. She tried, and that's all that matters to me. I make my way back to the door, noticing she's wearing real clothes today, not just the sweatpants and hoodies she usually wears when spending the day out on the farm. This time, I step right into her and brush my fingers beneath her chin, forcing her stare right at mine. I hold her there, taking advantage of her closeness. "Tell me, baby," I murmur, my lips so close to hers that all she'd have to do is close the distance. "I can't give you what you need if you don't open that pretty mouth of yours."

Her brows furrow, desperately wanting to prove a point, but she lets out a sigh instead, defeat flashing in her sweet eyes. "I want to come with you."

My brows fly up in surprise. "You want to come into town?"

She nods, going straight back to giving me the silent treatment.

"Are you ready?"

Mila nods again and with that, I step back out of the doorway, more than ready to show her off to the whole damn town. She makes her way up the pathway to the snowmobile I have stashed out front, and I'm not surprised when the walk remains silent.

I climb on the snowmobile, and she reluctantly climbs on behind me. I make a point of taking her arms and wrapping them around me.

She watches everything as we fly toward town, taking it all in with wide eyes, and I have no doubt that she's doing what she can to memorize the route we take.

A thought hits me that I want her to have the kind of freedom she deserves. I've never told her that she needs to be confined to just my property. I'm more than happy to have her wandering around town, getting to know the helpers and my parents. It's been her decision to remain on the property, and the fact that she's ready to start exploring gives me hope.

Bringing the snowmobile to a stop, I glance back and meet her concerned stare. "Do you want to learn how to drive this thing?" I ask her. "I have a bunch of them. If you knew how to drive it, you could get yourself around."

"Really?" she rushes out before remembering that she's supposed to be giving me the silent treatment.

I nod and indicate for her to climb over me to the front, and the moment she does, my dick hardens behind her. Having her so close every day and not being able to touch her has been more than a little challenging, and the contact erections are right at the top of my list.

With Mila tucked safely in front of me, she puts her hands up on the handlebars, and I reach around her before showing her what to do. She starts slow, and I won't lie, the first few minutes I fear for my life, but she quickly gets the hang of it, and I direct her the rest of the way, trusting that if she were to take herself into town, she'd no doubt come back to me each night.

We drive through the town, and as we go, she looks out at everything with a newfound fondness, getting slower with every second. "This is the local grocer," I say, pointing to the right before switching to the left. "Hair, nails, and all that beauty shit you girls like is in there. Also doubles as a bar on Friday nights and weekends."

"What?" she grunts. "How the hell does that work?"

"I have no fucking idea, but in a small town, people have a way of making things happen."

I point out our equivalent of Starbucks, and before I know it, we're coming to the very end of the street, right where my workshop is.

Mila brings the snowmobile to a stop right out front and simply stares up at it in wonder, and to be honest, I'm not surprised. This is generally how most people look at it. It's the very place they've imagined throughout their childhoods, but the movies don't do it justice.

"Holy fucking shit," she murmurs in awe.

"You can say that again," I mutter, climbing off the snowmobile and offering her my hand. "Come on. Let me show you around."

Mila doesn't take my hand, but she moves in next to me, standing a lot closer than she has the whole time she's been here, and as we make our way inside, I point everything out. The helpers stare in shock. None of them had a clue that I had her stashed away in my home.

I give her the grand tour of the workshop, introducing her to a few of the helpers I think she'd get along with before taking her down to the ground floor where the sleigh resides. Her eyes are wide the whole time, looking like a kid in a candy store, and I can't resist taking her right back up to the very top level to the vault and showing just how quickly she managed to get herself on my naughty list.

"This is incredible," she murmurs.

"I take it you're finally talking to me."

"No," she says, glancing away. "I'm simply playing nice to get what I want."

"And?"

"It's working like a charm," she says. "I'm here, aren't I?"

I can't help but laugh as I drop my hand to her lower back, leading her back down the hall toward my office. I won't lie, it's always been a fantasy of mine to fuck her across my desk, though something tells me she's not quite ready for that. Give it time though. She'll come around.

Reaching my office, I push the door open only to come face-to-face with my parents, the two of them gaping at me in horror.

"Ahh fuck."

"Holy fucking shit," Mila breathes beside me, gaping at my parents the same way they seem to be gaping at her. Only Mila looks starstruck while my parents look confused. Mila smacks me as she stares at my father. "It's Santa and Mrs. Claus."

"Yep," I say. "My parents."

"No one gives a shit about that," she tells me. "It's the real fucking Santa Claus."

"The fuck, babe? I'm the real fucking Santa Claus."

"No you're not. You're just some dude who took over," she says, stepping past me into my office and staring at my father in awe. "This is the real Santa Claus."

My father laughs and offers Mila his hand. "It's a pleasure to meet you, darlin'. It's been a while since I've checked in on you. Though I must admit, I'm a little surprised to see you."

"I bet you are," she says, glancing back toward me. "I take it your son failed to mention I was here?"

"You guessed correctly."

"Ahh," Mila muses just as her eyes begin to sparkle with wicked delight, and I realize this right here is the reason she wanted to come. Fuck the town and the workshop. She wanted to meet my parents just to drop me in a world of shit. "So, I take it that he also forgot to mention that he kidnapped me?"

Well fuck. She didn't even try to sugarcoat it.

My parents glance at me, concern in my mother's eyes, while my father just seems . . . unsurprised. "Why are you looking at me like that?" I ask, stepping deeper into my office and closing the door behind me, figuring that whatever is about to be said in here isn't meant for the whole town to hear.

Dad offers me a tight smile before dropping his gaze back to Mila, taking her hand and leading her to the chair opposite my desk. He takes the one beside her, and in that sincere way my father has become so famous for, he looks at my girl and gives it to her straight. "Oh, sweet girl. I know my son can be quite . . . difficult to deal with sometimes, and I'm sure you've had your moments of frustration, but it wouldn't be possible for him to kidnap you if you hadn't wished it into existence," he explains. "You're in love with my son, aren't you?"

Mila gapes at him, her gaze flicking back at me. "I . . . I'm too angry at him to be in love with him. I mean, I guess I am, but I'm really trying to focus on not loving him, and it's working really well for me."

My mother laughs and looks at me as though she's never been so proud before striding over to join Dad and Mila. She takes Mila's hand and holds her stare. "Let me tell you about the day this old buffoon kidnapped me right out of my bed in Colorado."

CHAPTER 16

NICK

JUNE

I don't know how the fuck it happened, but somehow Mom and Mila are best friends. They spend nearly every day together, filling each other in on the laughable stories about me. Only issue is, Mila likes to offer up a story every time Mom tells one, and considering Mila doesn't have quite as many, she's given Mom all the filthy details. Don't get me wrong, I'm so glad that Mila was so attached to the bright red dildo I handcrafted for her, but sharing with Mom what we did with it over Dad's birthday dinner wasn't exactly my best moment.

We're well and truly halfway into the year, and while Mila has definitely eased up on her silent treatment, we're still not where we need to be, but there's no doubt how happy she is now. She comes and visits the workshop nearly every day, and while she hasn't come right out and said it, I think she's found purpose there.

She smiles every day, and I fucking love it. She even offers the occasional one to me, and when she does, it always blows me the fuck away. I always find her checking in on me, whether she casually walks past my office, acting as though she isn't peeking in to see what I'm doing, or simply just being near me around the house.

She needs me, and while she won't admit it, I know that she knows it.

Mila Morgan still loves me. I just wish she'd be able to get past this anger that's engrained so deeply in her soul, and while it will kill me for her to ever leave here, if that's what she still wishes by the time Christmas comes around, I will send her home.

We finish up dinner with my parents, something we tend to do quite a lot now. I never used to. Every blue moon I'd head over to their place, and it usually had something to do with not being fucked to cook, but things have been different since Mila arrived. My father doesn't look at me as though he fears I'm going to fuck up anymore, and when Mom looks at me, it's always with a proud smile.

Tonight though, it's our turn to host dinner, and as usual, Mila stood right beside me in the kitchen and helped me cook a meal for my parents. And by help, I mean she eagerly listened to instructions, fucked them up, and needed me to fix it. She's a disaster in the kitchen, and I don't say that just to be a dick. I fucking mean it. She can't be left alone with a spoon, but I love that she tries anyway. And I love that every time she does, she always glances over her shoulder, checking to see if she still has my undivided attention.

The answer is always yes.

I watch her, but she watches me right back, both of us trying to be discreet about it, but when it comes to Mila Morgan, there's not a damn discreet thing about her. We've become in tune with each other's movements, to the point that we no longer need the strained communication. I can simply look her way and she knows what I'm thinking. Same thing in the morning, she knows that after I've had something to eat and a coffee, there's roughly three minutes until I walk out the door, and she always makes sure to beat me to the snowmobile to be the one who gets to drive.

There's no doubt about it. She loves it here. She's found peace, and yet I hate that despite how close we are, we're still so far away. I need to hold her, need to feel her lips on mine, need to hear the way she whispers how she loves me, but most of all, I need to taste her.

With dinner out of the way, I start clearing the table, and just as Mila moves to get up, my father puts his hand over hers, keeping her seated. "How are you, dear?" he asks, searching her eyes for the truth, a skill he's always been so good at.

She smiles, and I go about my business, clearing the table while doing everything I can to listen in on their conversation. "I'm happy," she tells him. "Really happy."

"But something is missing," he says. "I sense it in you. Your heart is still hurting."

Mila glances back at me, her gaze locking onto mine, and I don't even bother to pretend I'm not listening. "It is," she agrees, her words tearing me to pieces as she breaks our stare and turns back to face my father. "Don't get me wrong, I love your son, and I wish there was some way I could simply put everything behind me, but I can't shake this feeling that I was tricked into it. Yes, I asked for this, but I didn't have all the information. I didn't get a chance to say goodbye to the life I'd built for myself, and despite how much happier I am here with Nick, I still find myself missing the life I had. New York was where I grew up. It's where my parents are buried, where I became the woman I am. I feel as though I'm mourning a part of myself."

My head hangs low between my shoulders, not having realized how deeply she felt about this. It's so much more than I had imagined. I never considered the attachments she had to that place. I just assumed she was ready to leave because she hated her job and was lonely. She was a broken version of herself, and while that part of her is mended, I fear all I've done is broken a different piece that I had no right to break.

"I understand," my father tells her. "Life is . . . fickle. It surprises us in ways that sometimes we're not quite ready for. I think if you truly gave this place a chance, truly opened your heart to Nick, you will see this is right where you belong. You will find your happiness here, just as I have with Nick's mother. As for missing your parents and your home, I fear that will never change, no matter where you are in the world, but I can guarantee that it will eventually get easier, and one day, you'll be able to look back on those memories with fondness."

"I sure hope so," Mila whispers.

With that, my father gets up from the table before walking behind Mila's chair and placing his hand on her shoulder. "Do try to find it within yourself to forgive Nick. You both deserve to have everything with each other, and between you and me, Nick is better with you here. His heart is brighter, and I don't want to see what happens to him if you were to choose to go back to New York."

Who would have known my father was such a wingman?

My parents leave, and when Mila makes her way into the kitchen, intent on helping me clean up, all I can do is walk into her and wrap her in my arms, watching the way she sinks into me. Her arms wrap right around me, and as she rests her head against my chest, silence falls over us.

She hasn't allowed me this close in a long time, and now that I finally understand what's going on inside of her, that it's so much more than just being angry that I knocked her out and brought her here, I need to try harder.

"I'm sorry, Mila," I murmur, my lips against her hair. "I didn't realize it ran so deep. If I had known—"

"Don't do that," she whispers. "Don't regret bringing me here. I want to be here. I want to be with you in this place. This is my home now. I just need to work through some things first. But your dad is right. I need to figure my shit out, and the sooner I can do it, the better."

OCTOBER

My cock springs to life. These past few months have been fucking torture, and what's worse, Mila knows exactly what she's doing to me. Apparently, she made herself some kind of deal that she won't break during these twelve months, and she's determined to stick it out. Even if that deal was made out of anger.

She's not angry anymore, but that doesn't mean she's going to spread her legs and let me have my wicked way with her. She wants to make me suffer right up until Christmas when she makes her final decision to stay or go.

Fuck. Just the thought of her leaving cripples me because what happens then? If she walks away and decides she can't forgive me for taking her away from her life, what am I supposed to do? Will she keep wishing me back every year? Do we go back to the way things were when I would sneak into her bedroom just to watch her sleep on Christmas Eve? Not being able to reach out and touch her will fucking destroy me, but not as much as she's trying to destroy me right now.

I listen to her sweet moans coming from my bedroom, moans I would recognize anywhere. She whispers my name, knowing damn well I hear everything. She didn't even bother closing the door because she doesn't intend to hide this from me. Her intentions are clear—she wants to fuck with me. She wants to drive me wild with need, and it's more than working. Hell, I've had to jerk off eight times in the shower this week alone, and it's only Wednesday.

"Nick," she groans again, and this time, I can't fucking help myself.

Reaching up to the one cupboard she can't reach in the living room, I scoop up the little present I made for her earlier this week and make my way to the bedroom, pausing in the doorway, my shoulder propped against the frame as I simply watch the show.

Mila sits up in our bed, her spine straight against the headboard, head tipped back, and those beautiful eyes closed. She's wearing a black lingerie set with her knees up and her fingers pushing the material of her thong aside as she works her sweet clit. Her hand roams over her body, cupping her full tits before rolling over her pebbled nipple, and my fucking mouth waters.

I'm stiff as a fucking board, desperate to be inside of her, to be the one working her clit, to be the one with my mouth all over her body, but for now, I get my satisfaction out of simply smelling her sweet arousal in the air.

The very sight of her could bring gods to their knees, and as I fight the impulse to race to her and give her what she so clearly needs, I settle for clearing my throat instead. She opens her eyes slowly, not startled in the least, which proves that she knew I was here all along.

"Something you need, sweetheart?" she questions, only ever using that endearment whenever she's being sarcastic.

I grin and hold up the bright purple dildo, the exact replica of the red replica of my cock, something that took me three attempts to make. During the first attempt, the mold putty was the wrong consistency, and I didn't figure it out until after I'd stuck my dick into the tube. The second time, I took it out too early and destroyed the mold, and the third? Well, the third was fucking perfect.

"If you're going to sit in here and fuck yourself while pretending you don't desperately want to be a whore for me, the least you can do is ride my cock."

Her eyes light up seeing the purple dildo, and I toss it across the room, watching as her hand snaps up and plucks the silicone shaft out of the air. She's hungry for it, not having had me since Christmas Day, and this right here is the perfect substitute.

Mila wastes no time, crawling up onto her knees and settling over the purple cock, and as she lowers herself down, her cheeks become flushed, and I can't tear my gaze away from the sight. She tilts her hips back, giving me the perfect view of the way she takes the purple cock, and when she rises back up again, the silicone is drenched in her sweet arousal.

My cock twitches in my pants, and I have no choice but to adjust myself.

She doesn't tear her eyes off me, getting herself off on the way I watch her, and though it's not an invitation to join, she sure as fuck doesn't want me to leave.

"Fuck, Nick," she cries, her chest heaving, already driving herself right to the edge as her skilled fingers work her sweet clit.

She picks up her pace, and I can't take it any longer, pushing off the doorframe and moving into the room. Mila tracks my every step, knowing how much she's making me suffer right now, but judging by the need in her eyes, I'm not the only one suffering tonight. She's worked herself up, and now that she needs more than a silicone cock, I'm not going to give it to her.

"Nick," she begs as I make my way around her side of the bed.

I reach toward her, closing my hand around her throat and gently squeezing before leaning in close enough that she feels my breath dancing across her lips. If she wants to kiss me, all she has to do is close the gap.

"Nick, please," she begs.

"Come for me, Mila. Let me hear how you scream for me."

She comes almost on cue, and her desperate cries are like music to my ears.

"Fuck," she grunts, still riding the purple cock as her fingers trail over her clit, having lost a shitload of momentum in the past few seconds. She clenches her eyes and tilts her chin up, closing the gap between us just enough to feel the slightest brush of her lips on mine, but it's not enough to take what she really wants.

Her chest heaves, and as her orgasm fades, her body sags against the headboard, but I don't dare release my hold on her throat. She opens her blazing eyes, and I see the desire still burning within them. "When you're ready to be fucked properly, you know where to find me. But Mila, when you finally come to me, you better fucking beg for it."

And with that, I make my way into the bathroom, needing to take care of the raging erection between my legs for the ninth time this week.

<u>DECEMBER</u>

I'm on the fucking edge. How have we made it to December without Mila caving? I know where her heart is. I haven't questioned that for a while, but she held out just as she said she would, and now, time is almost up.

It's Christmas Eve, the one day that means the most to us, and it's now or never.

My knee bounces as I sit on the edge of my bed, my elbows braced against my knees as Mila showers. I feel fucking sick. There are twenty minutes before I'm due to make my way to the workshop and prepare for the biggest night of the year, and yet all I can think about is this.

She needs to make her Christmas wish, and I honestly have no fucking idea where she's going to go with it. Growing up, I always thought I knew her better than anyone, that I could anticipate her every move, but this past year has only proven that I don't know shit.

I'm losing my fucking mind. I can't handle it anymore. I've had her here all year, watching as she's fallen in love with my home, built lifelong friendships, and created a home out of mine, and yet she's never felt so far away. Don't get me wrong, the past six months have been a little easier than the first six, but I feel her slipping away. She's preparing to bail.

The shower stops, and a wave of nerves crashes in my gut, making me feel uneasy. This is it. The second she walks out of the bathroom, I need to know. Her time has run out.

The seconds feel as though they take a lifetime, and when the bathroom door finally opens and Mila strides out, wrapped in nothing but a towel, I see my whole world.

She finds me sitting on the edge of the bed, bypasses the walk-in closet, and comes to me looking just as nervous as I feel. She steps right into me, curling her hand around the back of my head, the two of us just being until I can't handle it a second longer.

"It's time, Mila," I murmur, lifting my head to meet her stare. "I need to know what you want. If you wish to go back to New York and build a life on your own, you need to tell me now. You need to make your wish."

Tears fill her eyes, and I prepare myself for the worst. "All I've ever wanted was to love you and be loved in return."

"I know," I say, reaching out and taking her waist, ready to tell her that I'll be okay if she needs to destroy me, that I'll find a way to survive, but we both know it's bullshit. I won't survive it even a little.

"I've missed you this year," she continues. "That's ridiculous, right? I've been right here, but I felt as though we've been living two different lives. I've never felt so far away, and I don't like it. Everything was so easy last Christmas back home. We fit together so well, and this whole year we've been strained, and I know I'm to blame for that. Perhaps I wasn't ready for the wishes I made."

"Mila—"

"Let me get this out," she whispers, taking my hand from her waist and squeezing it. "I know I started this year so angry, and it took me a long time to realize I wasn't angry with you. I was angry with myself, and now . . . I'm so confused about everything."

I stand from the edge of the bed, holding her to me, terrified that this is it, that this is the last time I'll ever get to hold her.

"I love you, Nick," she tells me. "I felt it the very first time we met . . . as adults that is, but I think a part of me knew, even as kids, that you were mine and I was yours."

"I've always been yours."

She smiles against my chest. "I've come to realize something," she continues. "This whole year, I've been so hesitant to build a life with you, and I was wrong for that. I should have put my anger aside, should have understood why you swept me away. You were saving me. I belong here with you, but I need to go back to New York."

My heart crumbles right out of my chest and I nod.

"Mila, please," I start, not above dropping to my knees and begging her to stay.

A smile pulls at the corners of her lips, and she pushes up onto her toes, gently kissing me. "I left my Christmas charm bracelet there, and I have to get it before I wake up on Christmas morning."

"Wait . . . what?"

"My bracelet with all the charms you gave me. I'm going to need that before I turn my back on New York entirely. Oh, and the red dildo. I can't have the purple one without the red one. It's a matching set, and we can't keep them apart like that."

"You're staying?" I ask, not giving two shits about the bracelet or the twin cocks. All that matters is her.

"Yes, Nick. I want to truly start a life with you. I'm done being a stubborn bitch," she tells me. "I'm ready to let you in. I'm ready to love you and really be loved in return. I want this, Nick. I want it all with you."

My lips crash down on hers, and she smiles through our kisses. "I wish it," she murmurs through our kiss. "I wish you'd never leave me alone. I wish you'd wake me up every morning with your mouth between my legs. I wish you'd make me come apart every time you touch me. But most of all, I wish that every single day I will love you even more. I wish to always be yours and that you'll always be mine. I wish to be the woman of your dreams and have the most perfect life with you."

"That's a tall order, baby."

"Well, I have it on good authority that my man is in the market of granting wishes, and considering just how much he likes to please me, I don't doubt that he'll come through for me."

"So, that's it?" I ask, never so happy in my life. "Anything else, your majesty?"

"I don't know," she says. "Just how soon does this Christmas wish granting begin? Can I put in for an early Christmas wish?"

"That depends," I say, and her body presses against mine. "What exactly is this early Christmas wish? Because I have it on good authority that your man doesn't need to grant wishes to give you exactly what you need."

"Is that so?" she questions, shoving her hands against my chest so I crash back against the mattress. She climbs on top of me, straddling my lap, and with a sparkle in her bright green eyes, she grins down at me. "Prove it, Santa Claus. Fuck me like I've been on your naughty list all year."

THANKS FOR READING

If you enjoyed reading this book as much as I enjoyed writing it, please consider leaving an Amazon review to let me know.

For more information on Santa's Dark Secret
find me on Facebook –

www.facebook.com/sheridansbookishbabes

STALK ME

Join me online with the rest of the stalkers!!
I swear, I don't bite. Not unless you say please!

Facebook Reader Group
www.facebook.com/SheridansBookishBabes

Facebook Page
www.facebook.com/sheridan.anne.author1

Instagram
www.instagram.com/Sheridan.Anne.Author

TikTok
www.tiktok.com/@Sheridan.Anne.Author

Subscribe to my Newsletter
https://landing.mailerlite.com/webforms/landing/a8q0y0

MORE BY SHERIDAN ANNE

www.amazon.com/Sheridan-Anne/e/B079TLXN6K

DARK ROMANCE STANDALONES
Pretty Monster (Stalker Romance) | Haunted Love (Brother's Best Friend) | Darkest Sin (Mafia) | Midnight Stage (Rockstar Romance) | Santa's Dark Secret (Holiday Romance)

DARK CONTEMPORARY ROMANCE SERIES - M/F
Broken Hill High | Haven Falls | Broken Hill Boys
Aston Creek High | Rejects Paradise | Bradford Bastard

DARK CONTEMPORARY ROMANCE - RH
Boys of Winter | Depraved Sinners | Empire

NEW ADULT SPORTS ROMANCE
Kings of Denver | Denver Royalty | Rebels Advocate

CONTEMPORARY ROMANCE
Play With Fire | Until Autumn (Happily Eva Alpha World)
The Naughty List (Christmas Standalone)

PARANORMAL ROMANCE
Slayer Academy [Pen name - Cassidy Summers]

212